On their first night Carrie
had been nervous, and Slater had
tried to think of some way
to make it easier for her, to
show her how fine and free
it could be.

But the moment they'd
stepped into the cabin she had
undressed, matter-of-factly,
a cigarette dangling from
her lips.

Her body was white and in-
credibly lovely, and Slater
had felt desire engulf him.

He had held her, hungrily,
and hardly listened to the one
thing she'd said.

"I don't think I'll be much
good at this."

She had been so cruelly right.

And that, in a way, was
what had killed her.

That, and a beautiful
woman named Jenny.

Alone at Night

Vin Packer

PROLOGUE BOOKS

F + W Media, Inc.

Published in electronic format by
PROLOGUE BOOKS
an imprint of F+W Media, Inc.
10151 Carver Road
Blue Ash, Ohio 45242
www.prologuebooks.com

eISBN 10: 1-4405-3702-X
eISBN 13: 978-1-4405-3702-8
POD ISBN 10: 1-4405-5606-7
POD ISBN 13: 978-1-4405-5606-7

This work has been previously published in print format by:
Gold Medal Books, Fawcett Publications, Inc., New York, NY.

alone at night

one

FOR ONE stunning half-second, as Slater walked through the snowy night toward Boyson's Café, he thought he saw the Cloward boy on East Genesee Street. Usually, it was Carrie's face he thought he saw in the crowd; it was Carrie looking out the window of a bus, or looking up from some table behind him, as he studied his reflection in a mirror, or in his nightmares—Carrie, the cigarette dangling from her lips, the slight tip to those lips, almost a smile of amusement, but really a thin little leer: *you won't get away with it, Slater.*

I am; you're dead . . . but still, telling himself that at such times, never quite took away the sliver of terror, at the unreal nearness of Carrie. Hallucinations . . . but still.

Only last week he had sent off a Christmas card to Cloward, at the penitentiary. If I can ever help you, he had dictated a little note to be enclosed . . . and O Mr. Burr, Miss Rae had looked up from her dictation with misty eyes which worshipped him, O Mr. Burr, to still forgive that boy, him—wrecking your life that way, drunk and O sir, you could teach us all about Christian forgiving!

Suddenly, as Slater Burr stepped inside Boyson's, shaking the snow from his gray-checked cap, he knew he could not face Jen's relatives that night. He could not face another of Chris' lectures about Jen's life being ruined, nor the nervous frivolity of exchanging gifts by the tree, nor everyone's asking him what the latest was about the plant . . . The latest was, he was losing the plant—Burr Manufacturing was going down the drain. Slater put his coat across his lap and ordered a martini. This time he saw Carrie's face reflected in his own eyes as he looked into the bar mirror; two tiny Carrie faces, two tiny cigarettes with their smoke spiraling up in his corneas; one saying, *'You're not a success without me, and you never were.'* . . . And the other? The same: *you won't get away with it, Slater.*

I've been getting away with it for eight years, Carrie. He picked up the martini and walked across to the phone booth. He dialed the McKenzies.

"Merry Christmas to all, and a Happy New Year!" Chris answered. That was Slater's brother-in-law in a nutshell: Mr. Goody Two Shoes, spilling over with good will and do good. Chris McKenzie, head of P.T.A., S.P.C.A., and last but O God never least, the Kantogee County Chapter of A.A. . . . Mr. Wonderful, spokesman for The Nearly Damned, available and declamatory any Friday evening in the basement of The First Presbyterian Church: My name is Chris McKenzie, and I'm an Alcoholic.

Slater said into the mouthpiece: "My name is Alcoholic, and I'm a Slater Burr."

"Very amusing, Slater . . . We've been waiting for you."

"Boozing it up over there, as usual, Chris?"

"I think you ought to search your heart and discover the reason you have to be so defensive, Slater."

"I'm just having a nice defensive ice-cold martini, very dry, with a defensive twist of lemon," said Slater. He parodied a singing commercial: "Remem-ber how great, all-thatbooze use-to-taste? Martinis—still do!"

"Did the meeting go badly, Slater? Is that it?"

"You're all dying to know, aren't you, Chris?"

"Jen was wondering, is all."

"Well put Jen on," said Slater, "and by the way, Chris."

"Yes?"

"I was in Cayuta Trust this morning. Old man Caxton seemed concerned about Jen. I wonder if you think that's any of his business?"

"I didn't say anything to Caxton."

"Right after he expressed his concern, he told me his dog had been sick last week. He told me what a fine vet you were."

"You've been drinking, Slater. You wouldn't make those insinuations, if you hadn't had a few."

"Yes, we're all out of control but you, Chris. You just let me worry about Jen's drinking, and my drinking."

"This is no way to talk tonight, Slater."

"It's the Christmas spirit, Chris-mess. Let me speak with Jen."

"She's across the hall at the neighbors. You'll have to hold on."

Slater glanced at his watch while he waited. Eight o'clock. The stores in Cayuta, New York, were open until nine on Christmas Eve. That was a lifesaver; he still had a few more things to get Jen. Things he could not afford. Caxton had been his last hope, and Caxton had flatly refused a loan for Burr Company. It was just too risky a proposition, with the new zoning proposal . . . perhaps some other bank, one out-of-town. And by the way, how was Mrs. Burr ("young Mrs. Burr", folks in Cayuta called Jen) how was young Mrs. Burr? He had heard—

"Heard what?" Slater had not been willing to let the thought trail away.

"O nothing." Caxton sang-song back, "We all think she's such a pretty little thing, that's all, and hope she's well."

Just across from Boyson's, was the downtown employment office for Leydecker Electric. Slater could see it through the pane of the phone booth, which faced Genesee Street. Even though it was Christmas Eve, and snowing furiously outside, there was a line in front of the office. Slater knew that if he were to go out and cross the street, he would find some of his own men in that line.

There were only a few industries in Cayuta. In addition to L.E., there was a macaroni plant, a shoe company, and The Slater Burr Manufacturing Company. The latter was the oldest drop forge factory in the country. It produced forgings for other industries, from automotive, to agricultural, to locomotive. The Stewart family had owned it for more than a hundred years until Nelson Stewart died, when Slater took control. He gave the company his name; he even changed the name of the Stewart-owned office building on East Genesee to The Burr Building. Even Nelson Stewart's only heir had had Slater's name: Carrie Stewart Burr, the late Mrs. Burr, killed (long sighs, sad eyes rolled toward heaven) by the drunken Cloward boy . . . . Slater took a sip from his martini, waiting there in the phone booth. I'm getting away with it, Carrie; it's Leydecker I'm fighting, not you, and not Cloward. He folded open the door of the phone booth and signaled for another drink. Then he fed the phone's box nickels, at the operator's time call.

Jen's voice was interspersed with the sound of the money ringing.

"What took you so long?" Slater asked.

"I was in the next apartment . . . with *drinkers*. Chris and Lena and assorted relatives are drinking ginger ale by the tree in the living room."

"I don't want to come over. Can I skip it? Meet you home?"

"You can do anything you want to do, darling. I'm bored to tears, and I'd love an excuse."

"I have a few things to get. Then I'll meet you home."

"I wish we could go to Europe," Jen said, and Slater knew then she was a little high; high, and back on going abroad forever, live on the Left Bank, on nothing—a loaf of bread, cheese, wine; what-do-we-need, we have each other. All right, all right, but not tonight, Jen, he thought; no patience tonight.

"If Leydecker keeps at it, we may go there . . . in rags."

"Wonderful!"

Slater felt his impatience quicken. Mrs. Burr spends quite a lot on clothes, sir, says Miss Rae; Miss Rae says, Mrs. Burr spent $508.15 last month, sir, and this month—

"Things are lousy, Jen," Slater said. "I'm not in a gay mood."

"How was it?"

"Bad." He imitated Leydecker's voice, "It is the *duty* of local leaders of industry to improve their properties, to appeal to local bankers, *if* necessary, for funds to enhance . . . Oh, well, it was that way."

"Chris said you saw Caxton."

"Refused," Slater said. "A flat refusal."

"But last summer Caxton said—"

Slater sighed. "Last summer, darling, L.E. was on the skids, and I was the fair-haired boy."

Only last summer, Caxton's kindly green eyes had looked up approvingly at the city council meeting, shining while Slater shined: "Don't think like losers!" Slater had shone, "Mr. Leydecker's attempts to get new industry in here are like attempts to get rich old strangers to change their wills in your favor! We're in the heart of the Finger Lakes, and we need to sell ourselves as a tourist attraction—sell our lakes, sell Cayuta, but don't sell it down the river to outside industry!"

"Winner" and "loser" were words Slater pounded in at

council meetings, pounded in with his fist on the table, his eyes flashing, huge and powerful, compared to little Kenneth Leydecker, Jr., balding and prim, his frightened eyes peeping out through his gold-edged rimless glasses.

Slater was the winner, hands down, in his perpetual battle with Leydecker. All of Leydecker's proposals—for a new municipal airport to attract industry, for a new zoning law which would force the Burr plant from its center-town location, for this improvement and that one, were fought by Slater in council meetings, and defeated.

Slater had only to remind Cayutians what had happened during the war years, when Leydecker Electric expanded via Stamford-Clyde, an outside industry, which shared contracts and labor with L.E., then pulled away leaving L.E. over-expanded and under-contracted, and leaving Cayuta an official "depressed area." He had only to call attention to the fact that Burr Manufacturing Company, built with local capital and local brains, had never employed any but local people.

Then, late last summer, the wind shifted. Oil wealth, a construction boom, and high temperatures in Kuwait, a Persian oil sheikdom, all worked in Kenneth Leydecker's favor. He won a contract to produce 30,000 air conditioners for export to Kuwait. Leydecker Electric, for so long floundering and fishing for new industry, was on its feet. The wage scale in Cayuta for factory workers was up—up and beyond what Slater Burr could afford—and the town felt a new hum, an upsurge in spirit: L.E. was working nights, as well as double day shifts. Kenneth Leydecker no longer looked like a loser, and the Burr plant in center town, began looking exactly as Leydecker always said it did: like an eyesore.

Jen said, "How about the zoning proposal?"

"I'm afraid it'll go through, Jen."

"Did you give them the arguments against it?"

"My arguments sound pretty thin lately."

"Did you tell them it'd put B.M.C. out of business?"

"That's not news to anyone, Jen, and it wasn't news to Leydecker tonight that I can't swing a bank loan. He's on the board of Cayuta Trust; he knows what he's doing."

"I'm sorry you sound blue, darling." And that was so like Jen, like her to tell him she was sorry, just as she might tell someone at the club she was sorry he had lost at tennis.

"All right, I'll meet you home."

"I'm so pleased! I was so bored, Slater! They're all talking about bomb shelters over here. Is that all America can think about?"

He supposed he was in for another evening of Europe versus America. Jen had spent two years in France, nine years ago. Life's highlight for Jen, Slater thought derisively; what she would remember when she was an old woman. And Slater? Carrie's face in the bottom of his martini glass now: *No, she won't remember her real highlight, Slater; it's between you and me.*

"They're your relatives, Jenny," Slater sighed.

"I never said they weren't. They bore, bore, bore me! I wish we could go to Europe, Slater."

"I know . . . I wish it too."

"And they're all eating! Peanuts, doughnuts, potato chips, just filling their faces. The fat Americans!"

"Okay, okay," Slater said tiredly; could he count 20 men through the windows, across at Leydecker's? 30? "God hate America."

"Well, I *do* get bored, darling."

"It's hard for an oriental like yourself to adjust," said Slater.

Jen giggled. "I may be an American, darling, but I'm not dead. Everyone here's so dead!"

"I'll meet you at home, Jenny."

"Pick up some champagne, darling."

Live on the Left Bank on nothing, a loaf of bread, cheese—

He said, "I thought *we* weren't going to make anything special out of this commercial proposition—*American* Christmas."

"We're exchanging gifts. We might as well have some champagne."

"Shall I get a tree? They're selling white plastic trees in Woolworth's."

"Yes, be sure to," Jen giggled again. "God, don't you wish we were in a little French café near the Seine, sipping wine quietly."

"Don't kid yourself, Jenny. That little French café would be just as hammed up with Christmas decorations as Boyson's Café here on Genesee Street."

"But everything would be written in French, so I'd forgive it."

"Joyeux Noël," Slater said. "Bonne nuit."

"I'll see you at home, darling."

"Au revoir," said Slater Burr.

Rich Boyson sat on a stool in the rear of his restaurant, waiting for Slater Burr to come out of the phone booth. Rich was not a localite in the true sense of the word. He had moved to Cayuta fourteen years ago, when B.M.C. was still the Stewart Company, and Leydecker Electric, affiliated with Stamford-Clyde, was the big industry in town . . . Even in those days, Leydecker and Slater Burr were fierce enemies, and Rich's customers had soon filled him in on the reason.

It was hard for Rich to imagine Slater poor, or working in the shipping department at Stewart—hard to think of him as a gangling kid without even a high school education, impossible to think of him as Fran Burr. (He had changed his name, after his marriage to Carrie.) But he was that, and he had been called Fran Burr, right through his teens.

It was not difficult to imagine Kenneth Leydecker's father keeping Slater's father on a foreman's salary, while he adopted all Roy Burr's ideas for switches and connectors to improve L.E. equipment. Roy Burr had died of cancer at 48, his savings spent on his dying, the family in debt at his burial . . . No, if Kenneth Leydecker was a chip off the old block, it was not hard to imagine that . . . And anyway, that happened all the time. Rich's own father had been a chemist, and Rich would like to have all the money his father's ideas had netted Canadaigua Foods . . . but Slater Burr poor?

Slater looked like the kind born to money. He was a good six four, one of those huge men with coal black hair and large dark eyes, sure and cool, with his checked caps and sports cars, and the distance between himself and other men, that made Rich call him *Mr.* Burr. He could walk into Rich's place in khaki pants and a T-shirt, and still there would be something about him to tell Rich he was better-off than most of Rich's customers. Not many of the better-off class came into Boyson's, but Slater and Jen did, always by themselves. They were the kind Rich liked, the kind who really enjoyed their drinks, sat at the bar sipping martinis and talking as though they were two youngsters who had just met . . . The fact was, Jen Burr *was* a youngster, compared to Slater, but Rich sometimes thought of them as no different from the university kids, who came over weekends from Syracuse or Cornell . . . Together, they were like kids. Alone, Slater was friendly, but not a talker, not one to sit on a stool looking around either; quiet, studying the mirror, a real loner.

The only thing Rich Boyson could remember about Carrie Burr was that she walked around Cayuta in pants, always with a cigarette dangling from her mouth. She was not a drinker, and during their marriage, Slater seldom came into Boyson's, except for cigarettes and a fast one at the bar. No one really knew Carrie. She had gone to school outside Cayuta all her life, and she had married Slater the first summer she was home from college. She was tall like Slater, with the same pitch-black hair, which spilled to her shoulders, straight and shining, and her face was not pleasant, because she seldom smiled, but it was a good face, Rich remembered . . . just very solemn, with brown eyes that seemed to look through a person.

But *Jen!* Jen was like Slater's buddy. Rich thought of it as having a wife who was a pal, as well as someone to cook the meals and raise the kids. Rich's own wife was married to the Motorola television set in their bedroom. Oh, she had had her little fling years back, and Rich had broken Al Secora's ribs because of it . . . but now her fling was played out on a 19" screen, marked out a week ahead on the *TV Guide*. When Rich got home at night and started to gossip about people who had been in the place, Francie could hardly tear her eyes from the Tonight Show. It worked out that Rich told her all about people like Slater and Jen, while she didn't listen, then she told him all about Johnny Carson and Zsa Zsa Gabor, while he didn't listen. Then side-by-side they went to sleep, each one feeling big-hearted about putting up with the other's drivel.

Sometimes Rich Boyson got fed up and told himself that if he were married to someone like Jen Burr . . . well, and he had to laugh . . . well, he would not be Rich Boyson, was all. He might be rich, but not Rich Boyson . . . He guessed Jen McKenzie Burr was the most beautiful woman in Cayuta, New York—hell, in the whole of Kantogee County! She was a little, very thin woman, with long yellow hair that hung straight and silk-like, skin like ivory, round deep blue eyes, dimples, and a snub nose. Rich thought of her as a little doll; that's what she was, a little doll, full of fire and what-for, and she could drink big Slater Burr under an oversized banquet table.

When Slater came out of the phone booth, Rich walked up to the front of the bar and pounded him on the back.

"Merry Christmas, Mr. Burr. Can I give you one on the house, for the Yuletide?"

"Thanks, Rich, but I've got last-minute shopping to do."

"Wish Mrs. Burr a Merry Christmas for me."

"O we'll be in during the holidays."

"Say, Mr. Burr," Rich said. "Know who came in here to use the phone today?"

"Someone who doesn't drink?"

Rich Boyson laughed; he stretched out the laughter. He had almost put his foot in it. He had just started to blurt it out, when somewhere in the middle, he had checked himself. God knows Slater Burr would find out somehow, if he did not know already, but Rich Boyson was not going to be the bearer of bad news. It was none of his business; he prided himself on staying out of other people's business, and for all Francie heard of his nightly gossip, he was clean when it came to keeping things to himself.

He intended to let his question get lost in his own laughter, then to shuffle away—fast.

But Slater Burr said, "*Who* was in using the phone?"

"Santa Claus!" said Rich Boyson, trying to sound as though he believed in the joke. It fell predictably flat and embarrassing between Burr and himself.

Burr responded with a thin snort, and swallowed down his martini. He swung his big legs off the barstool, and reached for his black wool cap on the counter.

"Seeing you, Rich," said Slater Burr.

Rich Boyson watched him push through the revolving door.

Santa Claus, he thought disgustedly, as he made his way back to his office . . . But still, he knew it was better saying that, than saying Buzzy Cloward was back in Cayuta . . . large as life and free as a bird—eight years later, using Boyson's pay phone, with his bags set on the floor outside the booth.

three

It was ten-thirty before the excitement died down. Its death left an uneasy embarrassment. The red and green Christmas lights blinked on and off on the small plastic tree set on the window sill of the apartment. The radio on the table played *O Holy Night,* and Selma Cloward, seated opposite her father and her brother, in the living room, glanced at her simulated diamond wrist watch. Her thoughts were spilling in every direction—getting to mass, what to do now Buzzy was back, and then on Oliver Percy, on why he would unbutton his shirt that way, just sit there with his shirt unbuttoned—period.

She said, "If you want to come to mass with us, Buzzy, it'd probably be all right, but you wouldn't have much fun, all girls and—"

"No, thanks, Sel."

His refusal made her glad she had asked. For the past hour she had wondered if she should chance the invitation. She was not attending mass with five other Ayres salesclerks, as she had pretended. She was going alone, and afterwards to Boyson's, and somewhere along the line she hoped to connect with Oliver Percy.

Selma Cloward was 30, three years older than Buzzy, and still unmarried. It was on her mind how Buzzy's return would affect her relationship with Percy. He was new to Cayuta, the new personnel director at Leydecker Electric. She had never mentioned Buzzy to him. He was a plump man in his late thirties, with a round apple-cheeked face, and bright blue eyes behind heavy black-shell glasses. A few weeks ago in Boyson's, when she was having the usual drinks with the crowd after work, he had come in, and they had struck up this conversation about winter. Right away, she had liked him, and nights she hung back when the other Ayres girls went on home, and they had drinks together. He was very much the gentleman, neat as a pin and one to order his scotch by brand. Martin's V.O., he always said, and his bills were never crumpled or old, but spanking new ones, as though he had just come from the bank.

Then last night he had asked her to his place for a drink. They had both had a lot to drink, and Selma had already decided on the stairs going up to his apartment that she would let him make love to her. She realized he was very drunk when they got inside. He had tripped against his table, and stumbled against the refrigerator when he got the drinks. They had three drinks while sitting on the couch, and on the fourth, Oliver Percy took off his coat, his tie, and unbuttoned his shirt. He pulled his shirt open and said, "There!" Then he took off his glasses.

"Well, you are quite well built!" Selma had said, for lack of anything else to say.

Oliver Percy responded: "I don't want you to think I did this because I don't think you're a nice girl. You are a nice girl."

So they sat there that way through another drink, Oliver Percy with his shirt open, Selma Cloward wondering what it all meant. At eleven o'clock he called a taxi for her, led her carefully down the stairs, and said, "Don't feel bad tomorrow. You're a good girl."

Well, drink did strange things to people, was all. Buzzy was proof of that. Selma Cloward loved Buzzy more than she had ever loved either parent, but she never fooled herself that Buzzy was not trouble. Long before he had ever met the Leydecker girl, he was making his way. As a youngster his idols were the Italian numbers men from the 2nd Ward, and he would run their errands for them, but late in his teens Slater Burr became his idol, and he picked out Laura Leydecker to make his way by new means.

Selma had grown accustomed to having her brother "away". His letters from prison were filled with talk of parole, but she had not counted on it. The truth was, she had counted on never having to worry about Buzzy returning to Cayuta. In prison he had worked in the kitchen, and taken correspondence courses. Selma had figured that when he got out, he would get a job somewhere miles away. In her mind's eye, she had seen herself one day years off, taking a train to visit him. She had imagined him older, gray-haired, stoop-shouldered, thin . . . meek, somehow.

It was true that he seemed more serious (glum was closer) and older, but his hair was the same fire red, combed in the elaborate pompadour he had affected eight years ago, and his gray eyes were solemn, but striped with a certain distant bravado, as though he were waiting for something to happen which would restore the cocky gleam there in the eyes of his photograph, on the mantle. He wore a light-colored sports coat with dark pants, and a jaunty, black-and-white striped floppy bow tie, loafers and red wool socks. He still had that habit of combing his hair every five minutes, then playing with the comb, twanging its teeth with his fingers.

He did have a job; he could not have been paroled without one, but to Selma Cloward's way of thinking, it was a very strange job for Buzzy. He was going to be a secretary to a man named Guy Gilbert, while Gilbert wrote a book . . . Way in the back of Selma Cloward's mind was the hazy suspicion that Buzzy might have broken out of Brinkenhoff . . . Still, he had written about this Gilbert, a newspaperman who had taken an interest in him. He was carrying matches from the Algonquin Hotel, where he had stayed last night with Gilbert. Gilbert had bought him the sports jacket and slacks. Gilbert had given him money for Christmas gifts, and in a week, when Gilbert came back from Florida, Buzzy was going to New York to work for him.

Maybe it was all the way Buzzy said, but The Whole Thing made Selma nervous, and for the first time since he had called from Boyson's, Selma Cloward was able to admit to herself that she wished he had not come back . . . Not when she was just getting to know Oliver Percy . . . just beginning to wonder how S.C.P. would look embroidered on the scarlet bath towels in her Hope Chest.

"Want some more wine, son?" Milton Cloward reached down beside the davenport and picked up the jug of grape wine. He poured some into Buzzy's glass.

"Thanks, pop."

"Wine don't hurt. Goes down smooth, don't it? It's not like the hard stuff. Now, you can hardly feel a thing, can you, son?"

"No, I can't feel anything."

"Not dizzy or anything, is that right?"

"I feel fine, pop."

Milton Cloward's way of showing intoxication was to get dizzy, a moment before he passed out. He seldom drank, only on holidays. He did not understand men who became wild and crazy when they drank, but he knew that it happened, and he blamed Alcohol for all Buzzy's troubles.

At ten-thirty that Christmas Eve, he was beginning to wonder if the wine had been a good idea. After all . . .

He said again, "You can hardly feel a thing, can you, son?"

"I'm really okay, dad."

"Yes," his father went back to the subject they had been discussing, "Cayuta's changing all right. Used to be the Stewart Building was the cat's meow with an elevator and one operator. But we got a team of six now, working two shifts, right up to eight at night, and nine on Fridays."

Milton Cloward was Starter of the elevator men. He was not a janitor, but off-duty hours he kept an eye out, like a night-watchman, which earned him the right to have this small apartment on the Burr Building's second floor. He could never get used to calling it The Burr Building; he had worked Car 1 when it was Nelson Stewart's place, and there were no other elevator men . . . Now The Burr Building belonged to Cayuta Trust. Slater Burr had lost it to the bank last year. Before he signed the papers, Slater Burr made sure Milton Cloward kept his apartment there; in the midst of all his troubles, Slater Burr thought of Milton Cloward. Another man—his wife run down by Milton Cloward's son, might have put the family out years ago, but Slater Burr was different from other men . . . Milton Cloward could remember when he was Fran Burr, a kid too big and busy for his age, and he supposed that was what made Slater different from other men, and he never had trouble remembering he wasn't Fran any more, but Slater—to Milt Cloward, Mr. Burr.

Selma Cloward said, "I'll say things have changed. Oliver Percy says we'll get more industry now, things are looking up."

"Oh yeah," her father said, "there's talk General Electric might move here, 'ploy about 300 men. Buy-build-boost Cayuta! See all the banners and signs saying that, Buzz?"

"Yes. It was the first thing I noticed on my way from Syracuse."

"It's hitting Mr. Burr hard, though. I hate to see that."

"He's paying slave wages down to his place, pop! It's about time he got it. Oliver Percy says he pays slave wages."

"Now, Sel, I told you that kind of talk ain't necessary."

"It *isn't* necessary, pop, but it's true. You can make more in the yarn department at Ayres, than you can make down to Burr's."

"Well, he needs to fix his place up. Repairs cost."

"He isn't fixing anything, Oliver Percy says."

"She just don't like Slater Burr's wife," said Milton Cloward. "You know Mr. Burr remarried?"

"Yes, I remember Selma writing."

"Married Jen McKenzie. Brother's a vet here now. Now, maybe she's a little hoity-toity, but she's a young—"

"A lit-tle hoity-toity!" Selma cut in. "A lit-tle hoity-toity! Har-de, har, har, har! She comes into Ayres like she was Miss Queen of England, and I can tell you I'd rather wait on Miss Queen of England, than on young Mrs. Burr, any old day of the week! She talks as if she lived in Paris, France, up 'till last Tuesday! 'Miss!' she says, 'I'm looking for a little envelope blouse, something to show off a seed-pearl choker. I saw one in Paris in shrimp-pink, which I adored!' . . . Oh, I can tell you, she's just what I need sauntering down the aisle on a Monday morning! And I hear she drinks like a fish too!"

"Now, now, Sel," Milton Cloward wagged his large hand back and forth, "that's just their way, rich folks. But I want to tell you, Buzzy," his face took on a serious expression, "Mr. Burr's been decent about everything. Do you know from time-to-time he asks about you?"

"He sent a Christmas card a week ago. Sent one every year."

"You see! Now, I don't want to go into all of That, but I just want the record straight. Slater Burr is a decent man, been decent about everything!"

"And Mr. Leydecker?" said Buzzy Cloward.

"Don't see him, s'all."

Selma said, "You know damn well you see him, pop, and he don't speak. For all I know, one day he'll put a bug in Oliver Percy's ear, and it'll be curtains for me."

Milton Cloward looked up at the clock on the mantle. "Holy Mackrel!" he said. "You see the time? It's quarter to eleven." He got up and reached for the jug of wine, carrying it to the kitchen. "I got to get going," he said.

Selma told her brother: "He don't speak to pop, and he don't speak to me."

"And Laura?" Buzzy Cloward finally said.

"She's a re-cluse."

"What do you mean, Sel?"

"A re-cluse. That's what everyone calls her. I don't know what it means. She don't come out."

"I know what a recluse is, but what do you mean she doesn't come out? She doesn't ever come out?"

"Un-uh. Never."

"That just doesn't make sense! Do you mean she doesn't go places, do things? Movies? I know she didn't go to college, after all. You wrote me that in one of your first letters, but—"

Selma said, "Buzzy, Laura Leydecker hasn't left that house in years!"

Buzzy just sat there, staring at his sister with a look of amazement. Selma Cloward looked away. She stood up, glancing again at her watch. She said, "Earl Leonard gave me this for my birthday last year. You remember Earl?"

"Yes. Sort of."

"We was going hot and heavy for awhile. I mean, it looked like the Real Thing . . . Then he got transferred, when the Wright Plant left Cayuta . . . That's what happens. We get a new industry and new men, two—three years . . . then pfffft!"

"What's the matter with Laura?" said Buzzy.

"Only thing I hear is rumors. She's crazy, she's sick— nobody knows the truth . . . I got to meet the girls, Buzzy. If we don't get there early, then we have to stand."

"Somebody ought to know the truth."

"Look, Buzzy, want my advice? Stay out of it! She sure isn't up there on the hill pining away for you, so just stay out of it! Want my advice, she's flipped her lid or something—I don't know. She's a recluse."

"It's been eight years. Eight years. It still affects her?"

"What affects her I don't know anything about, but my advice is, look what it done to you, Buzzy!"

"I haven't had such a bad time of it, Sel. Meeting Guy Gilbert was the biggest break in my life . . . No, I haven't done badly. It's just that, it wasn't fair. If I could only explain—just to myself, Sel—why Leydecker lied about giving me the keys to his car that night . . . then . . . then I'd forget the whole thing."

"I know you always said that, Buzz, about Leydecker giving you the keys to his car . . . but I been thinking about it for eight years, thinking about it and watching Mr. Leydecker prance around Cayuta, and it just don't seem like he'd be the kind to give his keys to a drunken kid he hated."

"I think he wanted me to kill myself, so I wouldn't marry Laura."

"Buzzy, that still don't explain how you got into Slater Burr's car. If Leydecker gave you his keys, you would have been in Leydecker's car . . . Naw, Buzzy, it don't add up. You was drunk, Buzzy . . . There I go again, saying you was. Oliver's always correcting me. Live around pop, my education goes down the drain . . . You should have heard Earl Leonard talk. Remember?"

"No, I don't think I really knew him."

"Maybe that's right. It was '58 or '59. Yeah, you wouldn't have known him. Well—pffft, like I said. But he was a talker. Propinquity, he says: that's why we fell in love, he says. It was propinquity. I looked it up and it means nearness. I always wondered if he felt so near to me, why he didn't ask me to go to Rochester, when the Wright plant moved. But he didn't. Anyways," she said, "I got this watch from him. And now . . . there's this new man. Oliver Percy. Oh, he's a gentleman . . . intellectual type."

"A recluse," Buzzy Cloward said. "I remember her hair. You know, Sel, in prison you read a lot. An awful lot. There's not much else to do. I even read poetry, if you can imagine. I remember this one about this farmer, married a girl who didn't want to sleep with him."

"What'd he marry her for?"

"I don't know . . . He did. Anyway, he used to lie awake nights and miss her, you know?"

"He had a legal right. He could have gone to court."

"Well, he didn't. He just missed her. And there was this stanza, I remember." Buzzy Cloward sat up straight, looking down at his hands as he recited:

> She sleeps up in the attic there
> Alone poor maid. 'Tis but a stair
> Between us. Oh, my God, the down,
> The soft young down of her, the brown
> The brown of her—her eyes, her hair, her hair!

He coughed self-consciously, reached for his wine glass, and took a long swallow. His sister was embarrassed too, and she coughed and murmured ". . . the way the cookie crumbles, I guess."

Buzzy said, "Between you and me, maybe I was never really in love with her, but I used to remember that. Her hair. That line: 'The brown of her—her eyes, her hair, her hair!' "

Selma said, "Well, her hair was her best feature."

"Yes."

"Laura Leydecker's hair was her very best feature . . . Other than that, she was peculiar."

"Not that peculiar. She was sick a lot. Shy too."

"Well, now she's a re-cluse."

"We used to have good times. I never minded the way she was."

"It's the way the cookie crumbles, Buzzy . . . I got that expression from Earl. He was a great one for expressions."

Milton Cloward walked into the living room wearing his overcoat, carrying his hat. "We better push on, Sel."

"I'll get my coat, pop."

"You understand don't you, son? I wouldn't leave you alone on Christmas Eve, but I didn't plan on you. Didn't even know you was coming."

"It's okay, pop, honest! I'm tired too."

"You just pull out that hide-a-bed . . . You know how it works? They had them things before you went up, didn't they?"

"Yes, pop."

"I didn't mean to say it like that."

"It's all right. I was 'sent up.' There's nothing wrong with calling a spade a spade, pop."

"And you understand about tonight?"

"Sure. Of course!"

"You see, Olinski's new on the job. Heck, he didn't have nothing steady working for him for years, you know? Watchman this place, parking lot attendant that place, sort of a drifter. Now, he's got something steady, something regular and decent. I put him on Car 2, right before the holidays. That's the most important, gets the most traffic. Should have seen his face, son! Well, when Olinski asks me to drop in on the festivities at his place tonight, was about a week ago. I didn't think I'd have much to do, so I said yes."

"I know, dad. I really want to get some sleep."

"Means a lot to Olinski to have the Starter show up to his place, you know?"

"Sure."

"Heck, all we'd do is sit around and sip and get dizzy. Be in no shape to open our presents tomorrow morning."

"Have a good time, pop."

"I put the wine away, Buzzy, but I don't want you to think I mind if you have another little one. Christmas Eve and all. But you know, too much isn't good no matter if it's whiskey or beer or wine."

"Don't worry, pop, I've had enough."

"I wasn't worried. Don't get that idea. You wouldn't make the same mistake twice, not after what you been through. Isn't that right?"

"Right."

"So you just feel free to do what you feel like. I don't think you feel like going out or anything, do you?"

"No, I told you. Thanks. I'm going to bed."

"Well, okay, son. It's your home. You treat it like your home."

"C'mon," Selma Cloward called from the hallway, "or I'll be late and have to stand, pop!"

four

" 'I do not want to be intimate with people. Why did I come here to a small town?' . . . Know who said that, Slater?"

Jen Burr wore a big, jackety lime-green cardigan, over white wool pants. She was barefoot, stretched out on her back, on the thick gold carpet in their living room. There was a black velvet pillow under her blonde head; her legs were crossed, and one hand held a champagne glass half-full; the other, a long cigarette holder carved from ivory. She smoked Gauloises, a French cigarette. The smoke spiraled up between Slater and her. He was lying on his stomach, on the eight-foot salmon-colored velvet couch, his glass of champagne resting on the rug by the couch leg. He wore white boxer shorts, nothing else. The room was dimly lit by the Solar lamp on Slater's kneehole desk; in the background Booker Little's trumpet sounded softly on the hi-fi.

Slater said, "Who said it?"

"Sherwood Anderson said it."

"It's profound," Slater said. "I wonder how he ever thought of it."

Jen giggled. "I love you, Slater Burr."

"Je t'adore," Slater said.

"You make it sound like 'shut the door.' "

"What time is it?"

"Eleven-ten P.M. Christmas Eve. Merry X . . . Do you know how Sherwood Anderson died, darling?"

"Nope."

"He choked on a toothpick."

"Hmm."

"Isn't that a typical ending for an American writer?"

"I'm sure we had a few who coughed themselves to death with consumption, in the grand European tradition."

"Are you in a mood tonight?"

"A mood for what?"

"A mood . . . You know. Depressed?"

"Not particularly."

"Good . . . God, I love Max Roach."

Slater said, "Who the hell is Max Roach?"

"He's playing the drums and vibes. Hear him?"

"Um hmm."

"I saw Stan Getz in Paris, just about ten years ago to-night. Lord, I remember that night! If anyone had ever told me that night, that I'd be living in Cayuta, New York now, I'd have jumped in the Seine."

Slater said, "Darling, when you die—no matter what year or where, I'm going to have engraved on your tombstone, born Buffalo, New York 1929, died Paris, France, 1952."

"That's not very nice."

"Don't make it into something now; it's just a joke. Just a weak little joke."

"I'm not dead—it's this town."

"Sometimes you talk as though I personally dragged you away from Paris by the hair, and brought you here."

"Slater, I never blame you. You're the only one who's alive in the whole damn town! I knew that the minute I saw you. I saw you across the room that night, and I honest-to-God fell in love with the back of your head!"

"I wish to hell we could get out of this town too, Jen. You know that, don't you?"

"I don't see why we can't. With Leydecker squeezing you this way, I don't see why we don't just sell out and get out!"

Slater hauled himself up from the couch. "Want more champagne, or have we had enough?"

"Please, darling."

He reached down for her glass. "I wouldn't get more than peanuts for the place, the condition it's in. And if the new zoning proposal goes through, I couldn't sell it even for peanuts. I'd have to merge with some company already set up, work for them. I'm 47 years old, and the only thing I know a damn about is the forging business. I'd be lucky to be a foreman in a merger. Burr would just be a subsidiary business. No one's crying for a 47-year-old executive whose own place went bust!"

"But we aren't bust, darling!"

"Jen, we're damn close. People are really beginning to listen to Leydecker. Any more industry in here, I'll be out of business. I lost 10 men last week to L.E. . . . If a new industry doesn't do it, the zoning proposal will. Leydecker's beginning to pick up votes, and I mean—fast!"

"Oh, you've always beat out Leydecker, darling, and you will again. I wish we were in Paris . . . right now."

"I won't beat out Leydecker. He's foxier than I thought."

"Besides hating you, darling, what does he want all these changes for? He's got his new contract. Why isn't he satisfied?"

"For one thing, how many sheikdoms are going to be wanting air-conditioners? He's got to worry about what happens after this job. Some of the industry he's scouting might use his plant . . . Hell, if I can just get a loan somewhere, I can fix up our place, get a status quo on the zoning, and find a subsidiary line for Burr . . . But—it's like dreaming. If it wasn't for Leydecker, I'd get all three, but he's boxed me in. He's scheming day and night . . . It used to be, a strike down at the plant meant money lost, and I'd fight to prevent it. Now, I'm torn. The more labor problems we have, the more unattractive Cayuta is to industry scouts. I'm getting so I'm tempted to cause a strike. I'm getting—"

"Sentimental over me, darling? . . . Come on, honey, it's Christmas Eve. Hush! I didn't mean to start it all up again."

Slater said, "It doesn't start and stop at your command, I'm afraid."

"Let's have another drink."

"I'm on my way for more right now. I don't know if we need more, but here goes."

"Since when have we cared if we *need* more?"

"All right, okay, more champagne, coming up."

"And no more shop talk, hmm?"

"No more shop talk," Slater said.

Jen McKenzie had initially come to Cayuta for a few months' visit with her brother. Chris was a veterinarian, who used to practice in Buffalo, New York. He moved to Cayuta after a scandal over the fact that he was selling, for medical experiments, the pets which clients brought him to "put to sleep." The near ruin resulting from the scandal had a sobering effect on Chris, whose very name in the same sentence with "sober" was a novelty. Chris joined Alcoholics Anonymous, and the Society For The Prevention of Cruelty to Animals. The toughest and most scraggly old cat handed over by a client, was put to sleep as delicately as one handled long-stemmed crystal, and anti-vivisection became Chris McKenzie's middle name.

Whatever thread of rebellion there was left in Chris by

summer 1954 squirmed uneasily around his sister in the presence of Slater Burr. He had been the one to introduce them, on a June night at the country club.

"Who's that large man with his back to me, Chris?"

"Slater Burr."

"And the woman?"

"Carrie, his wife."

"*She's* his wife?"

"Yes."

"Good God, I saw her earlier in the Ladies. I took her for a lesbian."

"Well, she's not, and don't shout that word around the club."

"Introduce me . . . to him, I mean."

It began then.

Chris did not know it then, and Lena never knew it. Maybe no one at The Kantogee Country Club knew it that night, but Jen and Slater.

Slater told her later . . . a few days later as they parked in his Jaguar up at Blood Neck Point, on Cayuta Lake: "I fell in love with you instantaneously, Jen. Was it that way for you too?"

"Faster than that," Jen had answered.

A month from that night, Chris came into the guest room where Jen was finishing dressing.

"Going out again?"

"And again, and again."

"I know who it is, Jen. It's trouble, believe me."

"I can't help it, Chris," she had told him frankly. "I don't know how to stop."

The Booker Little record rejected itself, and Eric Dolphy's alto sax began a lazy exploration of "Stormy Weather." Jen Burr rolled over on her stomach and lit another Gauloise.

"What are you smiling about?" Slater said, coming in with the champagne glasses.

"I was remembering a night at Blood Neck Point."

"Any one in particular?"

The first one."

"The night poor Secora got beat up for making time with Francie Boyson."

"That's right, we saw them there. They were leaving when we were driving in. You said 'Good God, that's my foreman with Rich Boyson's wife.' I didn't know how funny it was then. I was just afraid it'd be our first and last night."

"Boyson broke a couple of his ribs . . . You'd never think Rich was anything but easy-going. Tonight, I think he was drunk. He offered to buy me a drink, and said something about Santa Claus coming in this afternoon to use the phone."

"Our first night," Jen said, "and you said you fell in love with me instantaneously."

"Do you remember what was playing on the radio?"

"Doggie in the Window."

"Right!" Slater grinned down at her as he gave her the champagne. "I must have that doggie in the window."

"And I was thinking—I must have that Slater Burr."

"You had him."

"Not quite, darling, not at all quite."

He went back and flopped on the couch.

She said, "Slater? If things hadn't turned out the way they did, what do you think you'd be doing tonight?"

"What do you want to hear, Jen? That I'd be up in bed laying Carrie?"

"Why do you get so angry? You get angry whenever I bring it up."

"There's no need to bring it up. Why must we talk about Carrie?"

"Because we never have. It's been eight years. It seems to me enough time has elapsed so—"

"So that we can go into the intimate details of my marriage with Carrie?"

"I didn't mean just that, but that's a start, at least."

"A start to what? A fight? Every time you drink—"

"No, Slater, you know that's not fair. Not every time I drink. Hardly ever. But Carrie was—so damn unlike someone you'd marry. I could understand if it had been for money, but—"

"But it wasn't."

"I know. You've said it enough."

"I'm not in a mood to tell you what Carrie was like in bed, and that's what you're fishing for, Jen."

"There probably wasn't any bed."

"Then there probably isn't anything for me to say on the subject."

"I wish you'd just talk about her. You still feel guilty, Slater, that's what I'm getting at. Just because we wished her dead, and she died, you feel guilty."

"I did not wish her dead, goddam it! I wanted you, and I didn't want her, but I did not wish her dead, Jenny!"

Slater sat up and scratched a match to light a cigarette. "I wished her dead! That's one hell of a nice topic for Christmas Eve!"

"Should we save it for December 26th, or the day after Easter, or the day after Thanksgiving, or the day after Mother's Day, or—"

"Stop it, Jenny!" Slater shouted. "You're drunk, and you want a fight. You're bored, and you want a good fight!"

"If it takes a fight to make you discuss it with me, then let's fight. Turn up Eric Dolphy and we'll shout over it, if you want, but let's discuss it!"

"Eric Dolphy, Eric Dolphy, somebody or other Roach! I'll say this for you, Jen, you don't miss one goddam beat of the music. We could be blown sky-high by the bomb, and you'd know whether it was Charles Mingus playing at the time, or Thelonious Monk!"

"Carrie wasn't killed, Slater! You didn't kill her and whatever-his-name-was Cloward didn't kill her. She jumped in front of that car!"

Slater sighed. "Whatever-his-name-was Cloward would be happy to hear that," said Slater. "Why don't we wire Brinkenhoff, or whatever-the-name-is prison, and give him the news."

"Oh, you know the name of the prison. When I was in the office Tuesday, Miss Rae said, "Isn't Mr. Burr wonderful? Every year he sends that boy a card to the penitentiary!' . . . isn't that just wonderful!"

"So what? What do you want to make of that?"

Jen sat up and shook her Gauloise at Slater, knocking its long ash off on the rug: "Guilt! You're so guilty you identify with that drunken kid! You wished Carrie dead, and you feel as though you killed her, and not that kid. Well, I don't think anyone killed her. She couldn't stand losing you! It was suicide!"

Slater laughed. "Oh, God, you must be out of your mind, Jen!"

"I say she jumped in front of that car!"

"Out of your mind!" Slater laughed again. He tipped his glass over, breaking it, sweeping the glass aside on the table.

"And you pay penance! That's why Burr Company is failing! You're afraid to be successful without her!"

"Balls, Jen!"

"You're letting the place slip through your fingers, be-

cause you have to pay penance for something you didn't even
do! You can't let go of your guilt! That's why we're stuck
here, you have to pay penance for Carrie's death!"

"Jen, shut up!" Slater was on his feet.

"You'd think you ran over her, the way you act! Penance!"

In a long, sudden step, Slater Burr crossed to her. His
large hand cracked down across her jaw; the slap rang out
like a lash. Her champagne glass tumbled over on the rug.
She fell backwards, her hands covering her face.

For a moment, nothing but the lazy bleating of the saxo-
phone filled the room. Then Slater dropped to his knees
beside her.

He said softly, "Jenny?"

He pulled her up.

"I don't want you to touch me," she said.

Slater took his hands away.

"Slater, that's the first time you've ever hit me."

"I'm sorry."

"You know why I don't want you to touch me?"

"I don't blame you," he said.

"No, it isn't that . . . I don't want you to touch me,
because I want you to touch me. I don't care what you do, if
you'll touch me. Do you see what that's like, Slater? I hate
it!"

"We've both had a lot to drink." He knelt so that her legs
were between his. He leaned in to her and kissed her mouth.

She put his hands up to the buttons of her cardigan.

"I'm so in love with you, Slater."

"That's the way I feel about you." He undid the buttons,
reached his hand behind her sweater to the clasp of her
brassiere, and undid that.

After a while, he said, "Who's on the trombone?"

"Jimmy Knepper."

"I knew you'd know, even now."

"I love you, Slater. I just love you."

"Move to the couch? Rug's wet. Champagne."

"No."

The phone rang out and Slater groaned.

"Never mind it," she said, "Never mind, darling."

"Why do you wear pants? Complicate things."

"Why do you?" She looped her thumb around the elastic on
his boxers. "Off!"

Slater chuckled. "I do not want to be intimate with people. Why did I ever come here to a small woman . . . Know who said that, Jen?"

"Slater Burr said that." Jen sighed.

five

There was no answer.

Donald Cloward put the phone's arm back in its cradle.

He did not think of himself as "Buzzy" any longer. When Selma and his father called him by that name, it registered in the same nominal way most things about his old life did.

His memory of that life was very sharp, except for those few hours on the night of August 30, 1954. In prison he had relived his years like someone reading and rereading a novel, finding new things, re-examining old ones—viewing his life in a detached way, as a reader views a character in a novel, knows everything he can about the character, but feels no flesh-and-blood intimacy with him.

He stood up and ran a comb through his hair, while he studied his reflection in a mirror. He remembered once Slater Burr snapping at him: "Stop combing your hair!" and he thought of it then, and stuck the comb back in the rear pocket of his trousers. He was amazed to learn that the memory was still so sharp, that the inner punch of apprehension, still vivid . . . Today, he might have said flatly: "Why?" —he wasn't sure—but at the time he had felt as though he were stealing something, picking his nose—something, and Slater Burr had found him out.

Cloward walked across to the window of his father's apartment and looked out. Across the way the tower clock on top of the Cayuta Trust: 11:20 P.M. . . . In a way, he was thankful Slater Burr had not answered the telephone. It was late; what if he had awakened him? At the same time, he felt the urgency of making contact with Slater Burr . . . of starting the business he had come to Cayuta to accomplish.

East Genesee Street was lit by Christmas neons, and slushy now with a wet snow. NOEL chimed out from the bank's tower, and Cloward could see people in the streets rushing to church, to Boyson's, to The Mohawk Hotel Bar, to their homes and their relatives' homes.

Since leaving Brinkenhoff, he had felt as though he had been erased from life. He existed, but there was no life he was involved in himself; he was simply involved in other people's, as he encountered them, and not missed at the end of the encounter. He thought of last night at the Algonquin with Guy, the long torture of sitting there while Guy talked endlessly about Priscilla. Cloward had never even met this woman, never would, now she had run out on Guy, but he knew it was not the last time he would hear about her, just as last night was not the first time. The stories were the same. Guy repeated them, as though each time they were every bit as fascinating to Cloward, as they were to Guy. Hours dragged by. Cloward tried every tack to keep himself interested, and to believe he was a part of this man's life. Cloward asked questions about her, suggested answers to Guy's questions to himself, listened, listened, but each tack was futile. He was not even in the room; Guy was talking to himself: "My Cilly" this, "My Cilly" that . . . just as he talked about his work, with the same selfish force that believed Cloward had no life but through Guy Gilbert.

Cloward and Guy Gilbert had first met, a few weeks after Cloward had sent his recipe for Brinkenhoff Bouillabaisse, to the *New York Journal Times* Cooking Contest. Brinkenhoff Penitentiary began easing its regime at the time Cloward was sent there. There was a new warden, a more permissive attitude toward correction.

Cloward was assigned to the kitchen, a fact that irked him in the beginning. It was where the dullards were put to work. He borrowed cookbooks from the library. If he kept within the penitentiary budget, the warden permitted some innovations and experimentations with the food. Cloward had set out to impress the warden. He had perfected a soup made from fish and vegetables, copying the word "bouillabaisse" from a book which described a similar dish. When he read in the newspaper about the contest, he was sure he could seduce some outside interest to supplement the warden's interest in him.

He was not surprised when the newspaper's editor saw a story possibility in Brinkenhoff Bouillabaisse. Guy Gilbert, a reporter of human interest pieces, was sent to interview Cloward. Gilbert wanted to do a study of the Brinkenhoff correction system as well.

So it began, with Cloward believing he could use Gilbert.

When Gilbert helped him with his parole, Cloward congratulated himself. He accepted Guy's offer for work . . . Only in the past three days, since he was out of Brinkenhoff, did he realize Guy was using him, as a buffer against an immense loneliness, and as a sounding board.

The scene on East Genesee aggravated Cloward's feeling of anonymity. Next to the Cayuta Trust was The Clark Building. Eight years ago, on a hot afternoon in July, he had gone there with Laura Leydecker, to look at apartments. They were to be married at Second Presbyterian Church that September—never mind what Kenneth Leydecker thought of it any more. They had kept their bargain, waited one year.

Buzzy Cloward was nineteen that summer. He had gone through crazy years of wild-and-nervous carrying on. In those years, Slater Burr still owned the building where Buzzy lived, and Milton Cloward more than once spoke to Slater of Buzzy's wildness.

"If you speak to him," he would tell Slater Burr, "I think he'd listen to you. Tell him he'll never get nowhere, rate he's going."

And Slater Burr in those days, big and full of fun, easy-going and always warm with Buzzy, would take the boy aside and say in a stern voice: "Your father wants me to speak to you, Cloward."

"Yes, sir?"

"Well, I'm going to do just that!" still stern . . . Then, with a wink, "Hello, Buzz!" and he would pound Buzzy's back, chuckle and be off.

Buzzy Cloward in those days had been The One at Industrial High, which was not the same as being The One at Cayuta High, where college was the next step, and where girls of Laura Leydecker's class strolled through the halls with neat young men in jackets and ties, discussing This and That, not at all self-consciously.

The One at Industrial High wore work pants and denim shirts, put Alka-Seltzer in ink wells to the wild guffaws of other unruly boys (all boys), went to shop drunk on beer, and started sawdust fights from the shavings on the school floor, careened through the halls shouting and whistling, swallowing wine by lockers, flunking and repeating, and off-hours, stealing hub caps from cars, running errands for the numbers men, seducing 'older women' (girls in their early twenties who worked at Stamford-Clyde-Leydecker Electric), hanging around the pool halls and bowling alley . . . restless, attention-seeking, handsome in a rash, merry-and-worthless way . . . And always, the underlying gloom and fear of After Graduation, of girls who were not like Selma, but different and better, of running an elevator, or working at S.C.L.E., or wasting.

And sometimes, when he saw Slater Burr's sports car flip up to the entranceway of The Burr Building, saw Slater hop out, rich looking and unharassed, as though in all the world there would be nothing a Slater Burr might think to wish for, were he allowed just one wish, Buzzy would watch him momentarily with wonder: what could it be like to be him? . . . And Slater would wave at him and call his name—he always did—and for a moment, just an inch of infinitesimal time, Buzzy Cloward would be a part of that world which was Slater's, and he would feel the blood circulating gaily in his veins, feel some of the magic rubbing off on him, and a bounce to his step when he walked.

In his last year at Industrial, on East Genesee Street, at an Armistice Day parade, he saw a girl in the doorway of the Ayres Building. He was with Ted Chayka, both high on beer, and he stopped to look at her. Her back was to him, and her shouders were shaking, as though she were crying, and down her back, long soft brown hair, and she was wearing high heels and stockings.

"That woman's in trouble," he told Ted.

"It's not a woman. It's the Leydecker girl. She always wears those heels."

"She's crying, isn't she?"

"C'mon, she's balmy. I heard she was balmy."

But he left Ted, buoyed by beer and impulse, went up to her and asked what was the matter.

"I have an earache."

"My name is Buzzy Cloward. I'm an earache specialist."

"You know who I am, don't you, or you wouldn't have come to make fun of me?"

"No, I'm not making fun. I wanted to help you." And it was funny how easy he found words which sounded solemn and sincere, for part of him was standing off enjoying his composure and ease. He was an actor. "What you need is to sit down some place, rest a minute."

"Not in Murray's," she said.

He knew Murray's; it was where the Cayuta High kids hung out. He never went there.

"Tannemaker's," he said. "Do you want to have a coffee at Tannemaker's?"

She was not really pretty, but there was something winning about her. A vulnerability, and an intensity that seemed to know about it. Her hands were white as snow, fragile hands with long fingers, and a delicate look to her small, thin body as though she were made of porcelain. No make-up at all on her face, but these very clear green eyes, and lips a natural red . . . and tiny clean pearls at her neck.

She said, in that slow and well-spoken way of hers, "I don't think you've been drinking coffee," with just the barest trace of a smile.

"I will though, at Tannemaker's."

"You don't have to," she said.

"Your name is Laura, isn't it?"

"I suppose you've heard all about me."

"I'd like to."

How easy it was, and it never had been with a girl, except Selma, factory girls . . . not Kenneth Leydecker's girl or her kind.

In Tannemaker's he drank another beer, while she had coffee. Again, he stood off at one side watching himself there in the booth with her—the actor. For the first time in his life he wanted to change. Not for her, exactly, but he grinned at her, and he talked to her and made her laugh. He did not mind her strangeness. It was there, he could not miss it— not a balmy strangeness as Ted Chayka had inferred, but the feeling she was not following all the conversation. She seemed preoccupied and sometimes he knew she was not listening to him, and when she did listen to him, she took what he was saying very literally.

"I've had earaches myself," he had said at one point. "They're no fun."

"Fun?" said she.

"I mean, they hurt."

"Oh, I see . . . In yours, was there an inflammation of the drumhead?"

"I don't remember."

"I think I have myringitis right now."

"What's that, for Pete's sake?"

"Inflammation of the drumhead," she said.

He saw her often after that, usually at Tannemaker's in the beginning, and then, wherever they could manage. He was as odd to her as she was to him, but between them there was an imponderable rapport. She read poetry to him, and he, in turn, spoke words to her she had never believed were in the English language, and if he took her with a violence that showed his intense fury at her father, who called him "dirt"; she cried his name with trembling joy and spoke afterwards of his gentleness. They amazed one another, and there was that to bridge their differences.

At nineteen Buzzy Cloward was the first high school graduate the Cloward family had ever had. He was a manager of Woolworth's on Grant Street, earning $60 a week. He had a light suit and two dark ones in his closet, loafers, and thirteen neckties. He had stood up to the President of Leydecker Electric, and told him he intended to marry his daughter. He had been threatened by Leydecker, lectured by him, begged, pleaded with, scorned by him, and ultimately Leydecker had bargained. They were to wait a year.

It was a year which left Laura and Buzzy exalted and doped on the excitement they were able to create in one another. Marriage, with its license for all the more unfathomable-to-them opening of their senses and sensuous explorations, seemed to be the millennium. Laura was afraid she would die before that September, or that Buzzy would, or that the whole world would just blow up. The actor waited, patiently, pleased with himself and half-hating the actor, because he did love her, and told himself that over and over, watching for the change in Kenneth Laydecker's eyes, for the moment Leydecker would believe it, for the acceptance from him.

That day when they went to The Clark Building, there was still no change in her father.

Before they left the house, Buzzy said to him: "We're apartment hunting this afternoon, sir."

"I know what you're hunting, young man. Not apartments."

The superintendent was busy placing Fourth of July banners on the face of the building. He gave Buzzy the key to 4-F (furnished; $52 a month) and they both took the four flights by twos, by now both geared to Opportunity's magical and unpredictable way of presenting itself . . . Afterwards, Laura said, "I think sometimes it's all an illusion. 'All is illusion till the morning bars, Slip from the levels of the Eastern Gate. Night is too young, O friend! day is too near!' . . . Don't you feel that way, darling?"

"I only worry about your father," Buzzy had answered.

It was funny how the mind remembered little details, sounds and smells, so that it could summon them to life with the moment: and in prison, for Donald Cloward, that moment she said that, and he answered her, he was walking down the stairs of The Clark Building, and the tin guard on one step was loose, the stairway dark, smelling of lixivium and coffee perking somewhere, and from the street below a bus groaned. He remembered he had thought: This place is a worse hole than the place I live in now. He had thought of the spacious rooms in the Leydecker house on Highland Hill, the rugs and stuffed chairs and gold mirrors, room after room. And there was a roach on the stairway which he stepped over, so as not to kill. *Not yet, Leydecker; if I give you time, you'll come my way.*

"Don't worry about my father," Laura Leydecker had said. "He's resigned to it now . . . Oh, I do love this place— our first home, never mind it's tacky, I do love this place!"

Then, the glare of the sun as they reached the street; their eyes squinting in the new brightness, and the smell of paint on the clothes of the superintendent, as they returned the key. He was carrying a red, white, and blue puff-banner.

"Took your time about it," he said; he had winked.

"It was not a nasty tone of voice, I didn't think," Laura had said as they walked away from there. Then: "It was very good for me that time. Was it for you?"

It was another victory; God, he had given Leydecker a pounding!

But, "Yes, very good, Laura," and he took her hand possessively.

Donald Cloward walked away from the window. He sat down on the hide-a-bed, and lit a cigarette.

In a moment he would feel the hands on his shoulders again. He shut his eyes. He could smell August, taste whiskey, and in the darkness he tried to see whose hands those were on him there in the night.

six

He had never been to The Kantogee Country Club before that night, the 30th of August.

The club was set on Cayuta Hill, high up over Blood Neck Point, at the lake. It was a low-hung, rambling structure, with a red star attached to its roof. Selma's crowd, and others in Cayuta, called it "The Kremlin."

Kenneth Leydecker had suggested the evening—his first amiable move—and he had driven them there in his Chrysler. On the way, it seemed to go well, though Laura was very nervous, and Leydecker quiet, until the car approached the hill.

"The points of those stars are symbols, Donald," Leydecker said then. "Symbols, all four. They represent Character, Community Spirit, Culture, and Christianity."

Buzzy smiled to himself, remembering another way it had been put; he had heard it many times:

Character meaning born rich and look down
Community Spirit meaning pay low wages, own the town,
Culture meaning buy nice clothes, drink good booze,
Christianity meaning for God's sake, keep out Jews!

But sour grapes was not a part of Buzzy Cloward's mood that night. He said simply, "That's very interesting, sir."

" 'The desire of the moth for the star," Laura said dreamily, " 'Of the night for the morrow, the devotion to something afar.' "

"I don't know where you get all those thoughts, Laura," said Buzzy. "Do you, Mr. Leydecker?"

"That particular thought came from Shelley," Leydecker said. "All Laura's thoughts come from books. Laura reads all the time; too much of the time. I'd hoped she'd go on to college, and get some direction, learn to channel her intellectual capacities."

Laura said, "I have the oddest feeling of fluctuation in my ankle."

"You do?" Buzzy said.

"Yes . . . Look at all the crowds of cars. There must be 100 people here."

"Saturday night," said Leydecker. "You haven't been here in a long, long, time, Laura."

"I never enjoy myself here."

"We'll have a good time, Laura," Buzzy said. "Is your ankle hurting you?"

"It doesn't *hurt* . . . I don't read all the time either."

"I'm reading John Steinbeck's *Sweet Thursday* right now," Buzzy lied. Selma had it out from the Ayres Lending Library.

Mr. Leydecker pulled in at the parking area. Buzzy saw Slater Burr's Jaguar and said, "Slater Burr's here."

"Are you an admirer of Slater Burr, Donald?" said Leydecker.

"Oh yes, we're good friends."

"It doesn't surprise me."

"Sir?"

"I said, it doesn't surprise me."

Laura said, "I wish we weren't here. I would much rather have gone to a motion picture."

"Well, we're here," Leydecker said.

Buzzy had rented a white dinner jacket from De Lucca's on South Street, worn the trousers to his navy blue suit, with a navy blue tie and white shirt; black shoes, bought especially for the occasion. Kenneth Leydecker never looked at his daughter's fiance, without Buzzy's knowing instantly something in particular was wrong. Everything in general was wrong about the prospective son-in-law of Kenneth Leydecker, but each time they came face-to-face, there was the particular, always new . . . always clear in the beady eyes behind the bold-edged rimless glasses.

Leydecker said, "An ordinary suit would have done, Donald."

This conversation, while Laura was in the Ladies, to look at her ankle.

"Everyone is wearing white coats, sir. I thought—"

"Not with navy trousers from a navy suit."

Then Leydecker said, "What are you drinking, Donald?"

"Oh—" and for a moment he could think only of beer; he drank nothing but beer.

"Ginger ale and whiskey, I would guess," Leydecker said. "I believe that's what you people like."

"My people don't drink," Cloward lied; Selma always ordered rye and ginger ale. How did Leydecker know that?

"I don't mean your family. Your kind. Your class, Donald. I don't have to mince words with you. The people here tonight, yes, look around—these people are not your people."

"I know some of them."

"Slater Burr, perhaps, yes. Like finds like, no matter."

"I don't understand. You mean, because Mr. Burr was poor once, and I'm . . . not rich either."

"You're not poor, hmm?"

"No, sir. And I finished high school."

"You don't see anything else similar about *Mr.* Burr and you?"

"What?" said Buzzy. "What do you want me to see?"

"Take a good look at Mrs. Burr. Does she seem very beautiful, or gay, very popular? She's over there, at the table near the door. Look at her."

Buzzy had never seen her so dressed-up. She seemed ill-at-ease in the gown, and the inevitable cigarette hanging from her lips was out of place. She wore a large leather-strap wrist watch on her arm that seemed out of place as well. She was by herself, watching the dancers in the center of the room, with a certain bored air, as though she were wasting her time and resentful of the fact. But Buzzy had always liked her; he had never thought she was any different from anyone else—richer, and not as well-dressed as women with her money, but he had never pondered it.

He said, "What's the matter with her?"

"She's being used, I'd say. Ask yourself why a man like Slater Burr married her. When you have the answer to that one, ask yourself why he's so obsessed with seeing that his name replaces her maiden name—on everything—even on the building you live in."

"I see . . . and you think I'm that way?"

"I don't *think* it."

"Well, Laura and I don't want anything from you. We've never asked anything from you yet."

"And don't."

"Thank you for the drink, sir." Buzzy poured the rye into the ginger ale, then wished he had drunk it straight, though he was not sure why he wished it. He did not like the taste of whiskey, and he was unaccustomed to drinking it.

"It's the last thing I'll buy you, the last thing I'll give you. The first and last. I want that clear."

"I don't expect anything."

"Ho! Ho!"

"I don't."

"Wait until Laura's doctor bills come . . . You know, don't you, that among other things, Laura is a hypochondriac?"

"Maybe you've made her one, sir."

"We're discussing effect, not cause. Laura is a very complicated person. She's different from other girls her age, and she always was. You know she's different."

"We've been all through this, Mr. Leydecker."

"If you loved her—if—you'd let her have the chance to go to college, where her mind can be developed properly, and appreciated. She's very sensitive, a very nervous girl. You won't be able to handle her. You're nowhere near knowing her yet . . . Just wait. Watch her this evening, around other people. You'll see how well you know her."

Leydecker's bald head glistened in the light as he peered up at Buzzy Cloward. His small, bitter mouth was turned to a slant as he spoke, and he seemed to Buzzy like a weird, little angry bird, who wanted to peck out Buzzy's eyes.

"I know you hate me," the Actor said, "but I'll show you I'm not what you think I am."

"I don't hate you. I loathe you," Leydecker answered quietly.

"I don't care. I'm going to marry Laura." But his knees were weak, as they always were in a confrontation with Laura's father. The palms of his hands were wet, and he felt breathless as he stood there.

When Laura joined them, her father acted as though there had been no harsh words spoken. During the first dance, Buzzy said, "Well, he was at me again."

"Father is persistent. It's one of his major characteristics."

"He said he loathed me."

"It's so crowded here. I hope I'm not getting synovitis of the ankle joint."

"Where do you learn all those medical terms?"

"I just know them. I like to know what's wrong when I feel ill."

They danced the whole set, to "Hernando's Hideaway" and "Hey, There", "I Love Paris" and "Young at Heart". At the end of the set, Laura went back to the Ladies. There were many couples there their age, but when they waved at her (Buzzy knew none of them) she seemed embarrassed.

"Let's meet some of them, talk to them," said Buzzy.

"No. They don't really like me. I want to look at my ankle, besides."

He was not disappointed. He felt a strange exhilaration growing among the crowd of young people near the west wall, where they all sat in a gang. It was as though they were all witnesses to some imminent accident, waiting for it on their front-row folding chairs, holding drinks to tide them through the count-off.

A few times, meeting some of them had been unavoidable —in the lobby of The Palace or on the street, and always it was their amused countenances against the confusion of Laura, and a sullen defenselessness in Buzzy, so that Buzzy went away with the feeling that he and Laura were paired-off left-overs in life, mavericks of the town.

Buzzy wandered to the bar while Laura was gone, and drank rye without the ginger ale, a few shots. He saw Kenneth Leydecker, little and smug, standing at a table talking with the people seated there, rocking back and forth on his heels. He decided he would get Laura back in Leydecker's car when she came out; let The Kantogee Country Club go to hell! He would control her—he knew how to control her perhaps better than he knew anything else—and he thought of his hands on her, his mastery, the way her body went through every pace he put it to, the soft feel of it answering his commands, and then having her, after a long time, controlling her until *he* was ready . . . until *he* said so.

He had another drink when the set started, and Laura was still in the Ladies. He wandered back to the Men's. He combed his hair and washed his hands, feeling the Negro attendant's eyes studying him—his clothes. What did a nigger know anyway, but he felt a panic. Then, as he was drying his hands on the towel the Negro handed him, Slater Burr walked in.

"Hello, Mr. Burr!"

"Buzzy."

"Nice to see you here!"

"How are you?"

"You know I'm getting married."

"So I hear."

"The Leydeckers. I mean, Laura."

"Yes." Slater turned on the faucet.

Buzzy took out his comb. He began to comb his hair,

standing beside Slater Burr. He said, "We're being married in September."

"Umm hmm."

"We're going to ask you to our wedding."

"Fine."

"It's at Second Presbyterian Church. I don't know how big it will be yet. We have a lot of plans to make. Were you married at Second Presbyterian Church, Mr. Burr?"

"No."

"Well, Mr. Leydecker suggested it. I don't know how big it will be yet. We have to go over everything. I was telling Ken tonight, we want it just right." The "Ken" surprised Buzzy as he said it, and he was thinking perhaps he was just a little high. Then suddenly Slater Burr snapped, "Stop combing your hair!"

He stared at Slater Burr. Slater looked away from him, flipped a coin at the attendant, and walked out the door.

"I was just combing my hair," Buzzy said to the attendant. "Just combing my hair."

The attendant shrugged, and began rearranging the bottles of aspirin and hair tonic on his white glass tray.

Buzzy wandered back into the bar and ordered another shot. Slowly, all the while he was thinking over Slater Burr's flare-up, thinking over how he would get Laura back in the car, and how he was becoming just a little, very little high, he became very drunk.

It was not an unruly intoxication, not like the wild noise of wine drunk down by the lockers at Industrial High. It was a quiet, moody drunkenness, in which his words came out thick and lisping, and his coordination went off; he dropped a glass, knocked over an ashtray. He was aware at one point of Laura.

"I'm almost positive now that it's synovitis of the ankle joint."

He was aware of voices telling Laura he was in no condition . . . and at one point, aware of Chris McKenzie offering to drive them both home . . . and then, aware of telling Laura *she* could go, if she wanted to.

"I'm afraid I'm ill and must."

He stood at the bar and felt better, and soon, he felt he had a second wind.

Mr. Leydecker said he did the right thing, letting Laura go.

He smiled down at Leydecker, and he had a drink with

Leydecker. The hands of the clock above the bar whirled when he looked up there, and he grinned and told Leydecker time was flying, time was flying.

"You ought to go home."

"I know. I know."

"You can take my car."

"Oh thank you, very much obliged."

They stood in the lot, near a tree in the shadows, with Leydecker's arm around his shoulder. Leydecker was on tiptoe to accomplish it. Little Laura Leydecker's father; little roach he had not stepped on; little bird with button eyes— peck, peckpeck.

"Wait a minute. The keys. Is the way clear? No sense walking around so drunk, for everyone to see."

"Thank you very kindly, old sir."

"Not at all."

"See you around, old bird, and many, many thanks."

He sat behind the wheel. "Get in there!" to the keys . . . Singing, "Hey, there, you with your nose in the air. Love nev-ver made a fool—"

Somewhere then . . . sometime then . . . hands on his shoulders.

Ultimately—screaming.

"It's Mrs. Burr!"

Buzzy Cloward stared up at a million winking stars, whirling in a black August sky.

Then he looked down, and there were more little lights— a strange dashboard, needles, buttons, levers . . . A Jaguar.

"She was run over!" a voice shouting again. "Oh, Jesus Christ, she isn't moving!"

II.

With his fingers, Donald Cloward squashed the cigarette in the ashtray.

He stretched out on the hide-a-bed.

Once—a year ago? two?, he had talked about it with Guy.

"Guy, I know damn well someone took me from the Chrysler to the Jag. Those hands on my shoulder are as clear as—"

"Why didn't you remember it at the time?"

"Guy, I was scared! I just fell apart! I'd murdered some-one!"

"Spilt Milk Department. Anyway, you still drove the car,"

Guy had answered. "It'd still be manslaughter . . . Your concern is getting out of Brinkenhoff. I think I can expedite things, but I can't do it, if you brood over August 30, 1954!"

"All right . . . I'll concentrate on my typing and shorthand, and maybe next month, the warden will let me study dressmaking."

"If dressmaking will help you qualify for a job as my secretary, you're damn right you'll study dressmaking!"

"Okay, Guy."

"Just forget the whole business."

"Okay, I will."

But he didn't, and he wouldn't . . . not until after his talk with Slater Burr.

seven

"Hello? Hello? Good morning, sir?"

Kenneth Leydecker opened his eyes. There was a crack of light from the hall. Just outside his bedroom door, Mrs. Basso's shadow.

"A moment, please."

Leydecker scrambled out of the large double bed, and scampered across the chilly carpet to the Martha Washington chair. He took his blue-and-gray striped robe from its back, and wiggled into it. He was a small man, who often bought suits from the Ayres Boy's Department—size 16, usually—a thin, balding man, squinting for his eyeglasses now, finding them on the bedside table. Once he had them on, he got back under the covers, propped his pillows against the scrolled headboard, and leaned back with his hands folded on his lap.

"Come in, please," said Mr. Leydecker.

He was not a man accustomed to having his breakfast in bed. He liked to breakfast in the dining room, while reading yesterday's *New York Times*; then, on the dot of eight-forty, leave his home for Leydecker Electric, stay there as late as possible.

On holidays, he was acutely aware of his loneliness; he was lost and restless and nearly always teary-eyed.

Mrs. Basso carried a huge silver tray to the bedtable.

"Merry Christmas, sir."

"Merry Christmas to you, Mrs. Basso."

"The sun's out, and it's a nice bright day, after yesterday's wet. I'll pull the blinds for you, sir, and there's more Christmas cards on your tray there, beside your paper."

"Thank you."

"That makes 172 Christmas cards came for you and Miss Laura, so far, sir."

"So far? I should think this would be the end of it."

"Oh well, there's often two or three that'll straggle in the day after, and the day after that too."

"At least someone's paying attention to them."

"Oh, now, I think Miss Laura looks at them. I think sometimes when no one's around, Miss Laura looks at them, sir."

"Did she have her breakfast yet?"

"She was down early, same as always. There were dishes in the sink when I got here this morning."

Leydecker eased the tray over onto his lap, and put the napkin across his chest. "Mrs. Basso," he said, "there's something you'd better know."

"Yes, sir?"

"The Cloward boy is back."

"I know that, sir. My son told me last night. He saw him walking up East Genesee Street yesterday, carrying his bags to The Burr Building."

"Umm hmmm, well, I don't know what we can expect."

"No, sir, I don't either."

"Well," and Leydecker let out a long sigh, "well, Mrs. Basso, we'll just wait and see. Merry Christmas again."

"Yes, sir, and thank you for my envelope."

She went out the door, closing it behind her.

Leydecker worked at his soft-boiled eggs. Usually, on holidays, he stayed in his room, or downstairs in his study, avoiding the kitchen and second bathroom, and the hallway to the back stairs—Laura's ambit . . . In the beginning, he had done it out of sadness, kindness, and embarrassment, but now with the passing of the years, he did it to spite her, for he realized whatever brief and bitter encounter they had in the house was a source of perverse satisfaction to her. She would say the most wicked things to him, laughing out at his reaction, in her high-pitched tones of near hysteria, as though she were parodying all the scenes of madness she had ever seen at the movies, before her voluntary seclusion. Sometimes Kenneth Leydecker wished she *had* gone truly mad, but the wish filled him with contrition and self-accusation, for he was ready to accept the blame for Laura; if not blame, responsibility.

He could not blame himself for his intense reaction to Min Brister Leydecker's death. He had been raptly dedicated to Laura's mother; her death, when Laura was ten, had left him not only immensely bereaved, but simply inconsolable. He could find no sense to his wife's sudden death, nor any justification; there was only grief, and the numb acceptance of reality. As time wore on, he was aware of Laura, but he put her off. Mrs. Basso looked after her; he drowned himself in work, pleased and tortured himself with memories of Min, and Laura grew up. By the time he tore himself from the past and took an interest in her, she was behaving like some distant cousin his own age, with her spinsterly mannerisms and outfits, her imaginary ailments, and her nearly morbid addiction to reading. She was sixteen then.

Once he asked, "Laura, why is it that you don't wear saddle shoes, skirts and sweaters? Don't the other girls at High dress that way?"

"Yes, they do. I get a chill without stockings, and there is no support in those shoes, father. They're younger than I am too, you know, in their viewpoint. But I admire them; they seem very gay, filled with alacrity."

"Don't you ever mix with them?"

"I'm bound to, father. We have classes together. We're not close, though. They think I'm odd, and I suspect I am, from their point of view."

At such times he would think again of her mother, the same way he used to think of the dead as a small boy . . . as though she were just invisible now, but very much present and watching all of it. Often, alone in his room, he would weep and whisper, "But what can I do about it, Min? What? Show me!," as though the dead could show someone how to live.

He had an idea that college would be the answer for Laura. She was terribly bright, and he knew from his own college days at Princeton that the most incredible eccentrics often bloomed into astonishingly well-liked individuals. Radcliffe, he had always heard, was very successful with women like Laura, who were brilliant and withdrawn. He had once dated a girl from Radcliffe, who was now a leading physicist. She had married a Harvard scientist, and she was not nearly as well-endowed as Laura was physically. She had stuttered so badly, it was painful to hold a conversation with her; still she was very popular, voted something or other in her class, Leydecker could never remember what.

He had mentioned Radcliffe to Laura. She had seemed most enthusiastic . . . That was to have been the answer, and he had put her off again, suspecting least of all that a Donald Cloward would intervene.

Leydecker sighed and buttered his toast. At some point on this Christmas Day, he would have to go to Laura, and tell her Cloward was back.

Kenneth Leydecker had always thought of himself as a

Christian man, and hating another human being was incompatible with that thought. But he had meant it when he had told the Cloward boy that he loathed him, and he had meant for Cloward to kill himself the night he gave him the keys to his Chrysler. If he had not killed himself, Leydecker would have prosecuted him for auto theft.

Again, because he thought of himself as a Christian man (even as he walked back into the clubhouse that night, leaving Fate to decide Cloward's course) he believed that a Divine Power had interceded. Somehow Cloward had decided on a flashier car for his departure from The Kantogee Country Club (just give their kind an inch), and Carrie Burr had paid for his drunken audacity. Leydecker reasoned The Divine Power did not cause Carrie's death; it simply put Cloward's sort in perspective, removed any tinge of guilt from Leydecker.

When Cloward insisted to the police that Leydecker gave him his keys. Leydecker accepted the indisputable Scheme of Things, and lied. What would it have profited Cloward, had Leydecker admitted it? It would not bring Slater Burr's wife back to life; it would simply have involved Kenneth Leydecker unnecessarily.

Blood will tell; Min had always said that.

So it did; the Chrysler was not good enough for a Donald Cloward.

And then, it should have been that everything would go back to normal, to the way it was before that fluke meeting of his daughter with Cloward. Laura should have gone on to Radcliffe . . . to marriage . . . to the things a girl of Laura's background went on to. Never mind her bad start; it would have all been ironed out at college.

Leydecker squeezed the tears brimming in his eyes, and wiped them away with his napkin. Long, long ago in the old days, on Christmas morning, it used to be that Min and he would sleep no later than seven o'clock, when Laura would bound into the room, golden-haired and laughing, and tugging at their blankets to go down to the tree . . . Even after Min's death, there was always some polite and pleasant formality by the tree on Christmas; then breakfast afterwards . . . On her own, four or five years ago, Mrs. Basso had started coming in on holidays to serve him breakfast. It was the same time she had started her embarrassing habit of counting the Christmas cards, as if to say 172 people still cared, when the truth was: who did?

Leydecker got out of bed and put the tray on the bed-table. On his desk, by the window overlooking Highland Hill, were the files of the Boost Cayuta Committee, and the zoning proposal he was to edit, before presentation to the City Council. At least his presence counted somewhere. He was nearly sure of General Electric now. If everything else around him was suspended in some sort of lethargic limbo, the city of Cayuta would not suffer the same dilemma. It would die if it did, just as it had been dying before L.E. got the contract from Kuwait. It took a long time for a city to die, and in the meantime, while Slater Burr dazzled city officials with his eloquence, and the dreams of turning Cayuta into a summer tourist resort, Burr Manufacturing Company realized a nice profit. He paid low wages and put nothing back into the company. Even the Cayuta Fire Department was afraid to declare all the flagrant violations in the plant, for fear it would set the city in a deeper economic recession, with a shut-down of one of the few existing industries.

Kenneth Leydecker was his father's son, same as Burr had old Roy Burr in him. Leydecker could remember Slater's father, and the sniveling notes he wrote apologizing for days he missed work, like a child carrying a note to school after a day's absence. Roy Burr had been a pasty-faced, groveling man, too old for his years, always suffering from a cold and fits of lethargy, a huge, clumsy fellow with hairless arms and weak pouting lips, with a brilliant spark to his brain, imprisoned by the doughy layers of irresolution. His inventions were visionary, save for two which L.E. used to their advantage, and it was an incredible and imponderable discrepancy that this half-hearted, fidgety fellow had been capable of concocting any useful thing. It had been to Kenneth Leydecker, Sr.'s credit that he kept him on the payroll. He was of no use during a work day, off sleeping behind crates, watery-eyed from his colds and too much sleep, shuffling and apologetic, seemingly with only one wish: to die, and he had accomplished that at a premature age.

Ostensibly, Slater Burr was his opposite, a go-getter, wide-awake and angry as Roy Burr was docile, but the blood told as it always does, manifesting itself in a different and more lethal way. Leydecker had only to watch Slater Burr make up to Nelson Stewart, observe the subtle changes, beginning with his changing his name from Fran to Slater . . . then on down to his marriage with Carrie, his weak-egoed transfer of his name to Stewart-owned properties, his flashy accoutrements, and ultimately with Carrie's death and his marriage to a silly girl half his age, the gradual self-absorption . . . the drinking, and the deterioration of the Burr plant, the-hell-with-it slough-off of a whole city, behind a façade of concern . . . He was, in the end, as weak and irresponsible as his father had been; worse than Roy Burr, because he was a schemer and his weakness had vitality.

Well, and Kenneth Leydecker tucked his handkerchief back in his robe, with a testy gesture of resolution, he would rid Cayuta of Slater Burr, the same as he would rid a place of vermin. Slater Burr was just as noxious as vermin, to Leydecker's way of thinking, and sometimes Leydecker believed that if Fate had not dealt with Laura in the strange way it had, it could have easily been Donald Cloward he would be fighting now . . . And if Cloward's return meant he was to have two battles on his hands, then he would fight both of them!

Kenneth Leydecker dressed, studying himself in the full-length mirror attached to the back of his closet door. He was small and inconsequential-looking; his reflection mocked his resolution, but his jaw, his eyes behind the rimless glasses, the fists of his hands, and the tiny squared shoulders were determined. For he was his father's son, and Kenneth Leydecker, Sr., just as frail-looking physically, every bit as ineffectual in his appearance, had been a paragon of strength!

When he opened the door, and went down the long hallway, his step began to lose its quickness. His heart took a dive. From the banister, he could see the tree in the parlor, which Mrs. Basso trimmed every year, and he felt Min watching. He felt the fullness behind his eyes . . . the same old thing. But he pulled himself up to his full five-three, nervously wiped his mouth with the back of his hand as he paused before Laura's door, and then he knocked.

He heard the sounds of her television, as she turned it up at the knocking. Another movie.

He knocked again.

Louder, chaotic.

As he opened the door, the room was dark, but the moment he stepped inside, she snapped on the very bright overhead light. She was sitting on the bed, in slacks and a blouse, barefooted, wearing one of the Robin-Hood caps on her head. At the sight of him, she doffed it, in her usual exaggerated greeting, and dropped it on her lap. There was just a fuzz on her head; less than on his own.

"Please turn down the television," he said.

"You're standing very near to the set, father. You do it."

He walked across and turned the knob, lowering the sound.

With the remote control button, fixed to her bedtable, she raised it again, and laughed. "We must learn to meet Life's little obstacles with courage!"

"I have something to say to you, Laura."

"Oh, and is it Merry Christmas, father?" She laughed again.

"Donald Cloward is back in Cayuta," he said flatly.

She turned off the sound. She sat quite still, looking at her father, the shock registering slowly in her eyes. She was surrounded by the usual dozens of books and magazines on the bed, and by the small box of clay. On the bureau across from her, were scores of small clay dolls, all wearing brown wigs, made from the hair of her own wigs.

Kenneth Leydecker had, years ago, hired a woman to come to their home from Albany, New York, to fit Laura with a wig. She had come after a series of specialists had convinced him, that while there was no physical cause for Laura's loss of hair, the psychological cases were just as stubborn and hopeless.

Mrs. Tweed, the woman from Albany, referred to the wig as a "transformation."

"Oh, you'd be surprised how many women have to wear transformations, and no one suspects!" she had said. "Movie stars come to me by the dozens; café society, debutantes . . . why we had a little eleven-year-old girl last month, poor dear, not a hair on—"

And while she talked, matching strands to the fuzz left, explaining how to have a transformation dry-cleaned, and how to set one, saying "your transformation" this and "your transformation" that, Laura listened with no expression on her face. Mrs. Tweed worked four days, staying all the while at The Mohawk Hotel ("Don't worry, my line is top-secret, same as the F.B.I.") and at the end, she fitted Laura for two transformations, and presented her with three of the felt Robin-Hood caps, one in lime, one in bright royal blue, the third in scarlet. "For use when you're by yourself, or when you sleep," she explained. "The elastic inside holds them in place. It's fun to wear them at a jaunty little angle, and they come in all colors. I'll leave the catalog."

That was that . . . Laura never wore the wigs . . . She had already stopped going out of the house, long before the arrival of Mrs. Tweed. She would not even cover her head with a scarf for a breath of air in her own yard, and she did nothing to change things.

She stayed in her room, mostly, and if she left it, it was to eat in the kitchen during Mrs. Basso's absence, or to sneak a book from the library, off the living room. She had not set foot outside the house in seven and a half years, since the furtive trips to clinics outside Cayuta, with her father.

The few confidantes Kenneth Leydecker had were sworn to secrecy; and Mrs. Basso was . . . That was that.

"Donald Cloward is back, Laura," Leydecker repeated.

"Was he here?"

"No."

"Well, he's out. Free. So are the birds, father. It's hardly my concern."

"I just thought that you ought to know."

"Are you disappointed, father? Had you hoped he would die in prison?"

"To use your words, it's hardly my concern."

"It really isn't any more, is it? You haven't a worry in the world. Everything is in God's hands. Well, I just wonder what the hell God did with my hair, father! Do you suppose he gave it to some good little angel?"

"God had nothing to do with that."

"Yes, his mercy endureth forever . . . I bet you thank Him because there's no chance now of my seeing Buzzy, even if I wanted to. Do you thank Him, father?"

"Laura . . . Laura, I never thanked God for a misfortune."

"Well, give yourself time, father. Perhaps when you're kneeling down this very Christmas night, a little prayer will slip out. 'Dear God, all knowing and just, thank you that Laura is bald as an eagle, and not married to Buzzy Cloward, with whom she copulated in evil bliss and—' "

"Laura! That's blasphemy! Nasty-tongued blasphemy! . . . I did not come in here to gloat! What if the phone should ring, and suddenly you should find yourself speaking with him! You answer the phone sometimes! I came in here to prevent embarrassment for you!"

"Oh, I'm not surprised. You've always been considerate and attentive."

"I'm sorry if you can't see it that way."

"Why, if you hadn't been so terribly thoughtful and considerate, and kind, and attentive, there might be a whole family of little Clowards running around downstairs by the Christmas tree now, instead of Mrs. Basso. Oh, thank your lucky stars, father! It's much better this way, isn't it?"

"Laura, I—"

"Because we *would* have had a big family, father! Buzzy and I were naturals, father? Did I ever tell you we were naturals?"

"Very well, Laura, if you're going to start *that* talk, then there's nothing more I can say."

He turned and started out the door.

"At least I won't die a virgin, father . . . Put out the light, as you leave, please. I only put on the overhead light in *your* honor, father, so you can have a good look at me."

He flicked the light button with his finger.

"And a Merry Christmas to all!" said Laura Leydecker, as he shut the door.

"I think he probably has Blue Eye, Miss—Miss—" Chris McKenzie fumbled for her name.

"Miss Sontag, Dr. McKenzie. Mona Sontag. I work in the office at Burr. Secretarial." She pushed her empty glass forward on the mahogany bar, and Jitz Walsh put it under a beer jet to fill it.

"Well, I'm sure it's Blue Eye. Is the cornea a bluish white?"

"Sort of. Yes, and the white of his eye is all red. Poor little dog. We named him Burr. My mother did." She giggled, and turned to Slater. "No offense. I just been working there so long and all."

"No offense," Slater agreed.

It was late Christmas afternoon, near four. Most of the lake places closed in the winter, but Walsh's Place bragged: OPEN YEAR ROUND, EVERY DAY.

Jen and Lena were filling the jukebox with quarters, and while Miss Sontag solicited medical advice from Slater's brother-in-law, Slater sipped scotch, and tried not to get into conversation with the fellow a few stools to his left. His name was Secora, and he too worked for Slater, had worked for him as far back as World War II, when the plant was making precision forgings for airplanes and warships, and Nelson Stewart was still alive.

That day after Slater and Jen had their first rendezvous at Blood Neck Point (where they had seen Secora drive off with Rich Boyson's wife as they drove in to park) Secora had called to report his ribs were broken in an accident. Eventually, Slater learned Rich Boyson was the accident, but at the time he had shrugged it off without connecting the two incidents. He had ordered Miss Rae to keep Secora on the payroll during his long recovery, a gesture he would have shown any long-term employee. Secora returned months later with a chummy display of gratitude, which took the form of slapping Slater's back during Slater's rounds of the plant, and a few times, an invitation for a beer at the bar across from the plant, refused by Slater. Time passed and Secora's attitude changed; he was thick with the union leaders in the plant, less friendly, and Slater felt, slightly bitter at the bad times B.M.C. was realizing. That afternoon, Secora was bent on fond reminiscences of Nelson Stewart and "the old days," and Slater sensed he was working himself up to a fight, despite his euphoric air.

Secora was saying, "Those were the days! Say, Mr. Burr, did we win four Army-Navy "E" awards or five?"

"Five," said Slater.

"I was just starting in at B.M.C. then. 'Course, then it was Stewart Company."

"Umm hmm."

"We could sure use another war," said Secora, "or another industry in this town."

Slater got off the barstool, as Chris McKenzie was advising Miss Sontag to bathe her dog's eye with warm two per cent boric-acid solution, several times a day. It had been Jen's idea to come to Walsh's Place and bring her brother and Lena, to make up for Slater's absence at their home last night. Jen liked to "slum," liked crummy little bars like this one and Boyson's. Slater realized she enjoyed the attention she received from the people in those bars, enjoyed having them watch her . . . and perhaps envy her. That was part of Jen, part of her youngness and her restlessness.

He went back near the jukebox and caught a hold of her, waltzing her around the small space with an exaggerated aplomb. McKenzie's wife drifted back to the bar.

"Hey, Slater, it's a Twist, not a Waltz." Jen laughed.

"Only one knows the difference is Chris. He's the only one drinking ginger ale."

"Be nice to him, though, hmm? It's Christmas."

"Oh, I'll be darling to him."

"Having a good time?"

"Divine, Jenny, a divine time!"

Jen grinned up at him. "I know. But we have to make some effort with them, once a year anyway . . . and it's more fun out here, than in their place. Lena doesn't think so. 'Jen,' she said to me, 'you and Slater pick the lowest places. I mean, the people here.' "

"Too close to home."

"Don't I know it! Do you know she used to date Jitz Walsh?"

For awhile, they danced without talking. Slater's mind was back on Leydecker. The latest was that Leydecker had called an emergency meeting of the zoning board for next Tuesday. He was determined to push through his proposal. G.E. was ready to scout Cayuta some time in the spring, and it was Leydecker's thought that by then, a demolition crew might already have in progress the removal of the Burr plant. A park could take its place—a beautiful park, for public use, landscaped and lovely, in center town. The mayor had called Slater that morning to tell him about the meeting. The Cayuta Macaroni plant was owned by the mayor's brother, who wanted a new industry kept out just as badly as Slater did. It was an indisputable fact that Slater's plant was not only an eyesore, but also a source of labor disputes and unrest—another bad mark for the city. No company wanted to move in on trouble, but if the zoning proposal were passed, the trouble would be removed.

The mayor had said, "We've got to appeal on the basis that B.M.C. is a local business, and no city progresses by putting its own people out and letting in outsiders . . . Now, that's the approach, but it'll take a lot of fast talk, and you've got to work on a loan and promise great improvements via it. I can't fight, Slater. I'm in no position to, and it'd look bad if my brother fought, so it's up to you! You've got to stop Leydecker!"

"A penny?" Jen said.

"Oh, I was just thinking about . . ." Slater began, but stopped short. The door had opened and closed, and Donald Cloward stood by the cigarette machine, at the entrance to Walsh's.

"What's the matter, Slater?" Jen said. "See a ghost?" . . . Then she saw him too.

For a moment, he watched Slater and Jen; then, when they saw him, he gave a slight nod, and went across to sit by Secora.

"The Cloward boy!" Jen said. "My God in heaven! What's he doing out?"

"I don't know."

They kept on dancing, watching while Cloward ordered a beer, and Lena McKenzie moved away from him. Chris nodded at him, and Secora punched him in the arm with a big grin and asked him when he got sprung. Cloward's face went red with embarrassment. Again, he glanced over his shoulder at Jen and Slater.

"Let's say hello to him, Slater."

"What for?"

"What do you send him Christmas cards for? To be nice."

"Oh, hell—nice!"

"He keeps looking at us, Slater. Let's!"

She took the lead, and Slater followed.

Cloward stood up and made a jerky little bow. "Hello. You're—" and for a moment the words stuck in his throat. "You're—Mrs. Burr."

"Yes. How are you?"

"Oh, I'm all right, thanks." Then—and there seemed to be some special significance attached to the greeting and the look in Cloward's eyes, he said to Slater, "Hello there, Mr. Burr. I'm glad to see you again."

"Buzzy."

Secora was watching the whole moment with open curiosity, turning on the stool, and staring at the trio. Chris McKenzie was noticing out of the corner of his eye, still talking about antibiotic treatment for Blue Eye in a dog. Lena was lurking behind her husband, and Jitz Walsh had turned on the water in the bar sink full force, and was rattling glasses busily and nervously. The only one disinterested seemed to be Miss Sontag, who was trying to get Chris to help her remember the word "terramycin."

Jen said, "Are you home for good now?"

"No, ma'am. Just for a few days. I'm going to work in New York City, I think." He looked back at Slater, standing behind Jen.

"Oh, I envy you!" said Jen. "I adore New York!"

Cloward picked up his beer glass, and before he swallowed, tipped it slightly in Jen's direction. "Well, Merry Christmas."

"Merry Christmas to you . . . is it Fuzzy?"

"Buzzy . . . I'm called Donald nowadays."

"Donald. Merry Christmas, Donald."

Slater excused himself and went back into the Men's. He leaned against the sink, pausing to collect his thoughts. He was just a little tight, but he knew he should have been more effusive, should have pumped the boy's arm in the old gesture of bygones-be-bygones . . . was that right?

The shock at seeing Cloward so suddenly had thrown him off. He should have feigned the attitude of forgiveness, just as he always went out of his way to ask old man Cloward how Donald was, and to send the Christmas cards each year. He remembered the stumbling, remorseful letter Cloward had sent from Brinkenhoff the first year, and the agonized expression on Cloward's face when Slater confronted him on the night of August 30th. The events of the night began to whirl through Slater's brain, beginning with Carrie saying:

II.

"Actually, I was thinking of a way to increase the velocity of the power hammer, on the Rolli machine."

They were standing near the parking lot at The Kantogee Country Club, off to the right, on the bank, where there was a sudden drop to the highway.

He had seen her leave the clubhouse, while he was at the bar talking with Jen. Jen was telling him that it was hopeless; she was making arrangements to go back to Paris to work, and he was trying to keep his voice down, trying, without moving his lips, to tell Jen he loved her, his eyes looking away from her as though it were merely a quiet conversation, not the desperate intense moment it was, when he saw Carrie leave. He saw her face in profile, the cigarette in her mouth, the hunched-over posture he had found so endearing and sad, so long ago, her awkward walk in the long dress (her awkwardness too, he had always found dear and winning) and the solemn paleness of her face. She was furious, he knew; liable to take the car and go, if she were in such a mood, and it would cause gossip, inspire Jen to go ahead all the quicker with her departure plans . . . so he had excused himself from Jen and followed Carrie. When he caught up with her, he asked her if everything were all right. She gave him her usual shrug, looking off in the direction of the lake, not speaking to him. Then he had said: "What are you thinking?"

It was her usual answer too, to any attempt on his part to probe her mind. She considered her evasiveness a part of her immense control; it was Carrie's conceit that she never raised her voice, spoke an angry word, or discussed anything which bothered her, other than something like increasing a power hammer's velocity.

There were times when she would weep, but she would always have some strange explanation for it: her desk in the solarium was in the wrong place, or her cactus plant was dead (she was a specialist in cacti), and then she would do something about it, move the desk, bury the dead cactus, and the tears would be gone as suddenly as they had come . . . and the iron control back, the stiff expression on her face, the spring of vitality in her movements, as she drove herself through a day.

When Slater had first met Carrie, she was home on vacation from college. Slater was managing the Stewart Company plant, and Carrie had appeared one afternoon by herself to look over the machinery. Mechanics fascinated her; and her attitude, as Slater showed her about, was very much like a man's, poking and fooling with this part, adjusting that one, inquiring in her technical way about the use of the lever on one machine, or the roller on another. She wore fly-front pants and a white shirt, rolled to the elbows, showing firm-muscled white arms, and her stride as she went through the plant was long and sure, and over the shirt she wore a suede tunic, a pack of cigarettes stuck in one pocket of the tunic. Her face was marvelously handsome; a tinge of pink lipstick on very wide lips, deep brown eyes, a good nose, and black eyelashes, long and dark in contrast to the fair and perfect skin. As Slater had watched her, his heartbeat was deep and powerful; it seemed to him like some thrilling secret that her soft woman's breasts must be buttoned up in the shirt, covered with the suede tunic, that all of her softness and tender flesh in hiding that way was all the more intriguing and lovely than girls who showed themselves more daringly, as if to offer for approval what she took for granted and covered. So he told himself, and his blood burned. His excitement at that first encounter was at a pitch that stayed through all the other meetings with her. And he liked the way she was so natural on her tours through the plant, and the way the men liked her, not one of them fresh or disrespectful to Miss Carrie. He would hear them talk about her afterwards, all the talk admiring and amiable, as though she were a woman who cut through the vulgar and unnecessary underbrush of male-female differences, and class differences, and was simply liked for herself; not the way it should be with every woman, but the way it was around Carrie: her special individuality.

There had never been a single doubt in Slater's mind that Carrie was a fascinating woman; his marriage had endured for the sole reason she was so fascinating, but she was not vulnerable as he had once imagined when he was younger and had thought of the soft white breasts behind the tunic, white and unseen, waiting to be awakened; nor was she sad and needing protection, behind the façade of surety. She was a force, to whatever end, she was one.

That night in August, wearing the pink-and-white dotted chiffon she looked uncomfortable in, there was the same quality of wistful awkwardness and defenselessness, but Slater saw through the mask. He said quite flatly, "Carrie, you know very well about Jen and me, don't you?"

"Yes," she answered.

"Carrie, I'm going to say something that has to be said, much as you hate this kind of personal discussion. I'm very deeply in love with Jen."

"I'm not surprised," she said, not at all abashed. A slice of orange moon in the summer sky showed a placid, cool look on her face. She dropped her cigarette butt on the gravel and erased its hot ash with the tip of her evening slipper. From her beaded bag, she took another cigarette, ignoring Slater's fumbling for his lighter, and lit the cigarette with her own.

Slater said, "Is that all you have to say . . . that it doesn't surprise you?"

"Yes . . . That, and that I'd like to go home. Incidentally, Slater, the Cloward boy is back there in Kenneth Leydecker's car. He's very intoxicated. I saw Leydecker give him the keys. Leydecker must be out of his mind. The boy can't drive in his condition. We'd better drop him on our way."

"Carrie," Slater said, "don't skip over this one. Not this one!"

"I'm not skipping over it. I heard you."

"And you have no reaction to the fact I love someone else?"

She gave him a polite smile. "I don't really believe in love. It's a convenient word, one of those words which can force chaos into a more traditional pattern, at least ostensibly."

"I want to talk about it, Carrie, not around it—about it. I don't know what all this crap means . . . convenience and chaos! What does all that crap mean?"

She said, "If a man says he's deeply in love with someone, it gives him a more traditional license to behave as he intends to anyway."

"And when I was in love with you?"

"You intended to marry me, didn't you?" said Carrie. "It wouldn't have been easy for you to marry me, without saying that you were in love. I didn't require your avowal of love, but you required it of yourself. It was easier for you to believe it, or at least to say it, whether you believed it or not."

"I loved you when I married you, Carrie."

"We don't have to get psychosemantic about it. We're married, and that's that."

"You used to say you loved me."

"You wanted to hear it, Slater. You used to remark how awkward I seemed saying it . . . No, I was never comfortable with the word 'love'; you were right."

Slater said, "Then what did you marry me for?"

"I thought we would be good together, that simple."

"Good *how*? In bed?" Slater gave a bitter chuckle.

"I'm sorry if bed was a disappointment. I know I didn't place much emphasis on it, but I never refused you, Slater."

"There's more to it than not refusing me, Carrie."

"I don't doubt it, but there never was for me. Either way, it never seemed a problem to me."

"You could take it, or leave it alone."

"Yes."

Then she said, "It doesn't come as a surprise to you, Slater. We've been married 14 years, so don't act as though this is the moment of truth, simply because it's never been discussed between us . . . I'm quite serious about the hammer on the Rolli. I want to draw up some plans, speak with Secora on Monday. Will you drive me home now?"

"Some goddamned marriage!"

"I doubt that anyone's is perfect."

"I doubt it too, Carrie, but now I want a little more than what we have."

"You've found ways before, to have more than what we have."

"You knew about the other women too?"

"I presumed something like that went on during your trips."

"Did you know about Caxton's niece? That went on right under your nose, here in Cayuta."

"Yes. I received one of those nasty anonymous phone calls that fall."

"And you didn't give a damn?"

"I haven't been unhappy with you, put it that way, Slater."

"You should have been, if you'd had feelings."

She took a drag on her cigarette; the smoke spiraled up between them, and she said: "I should have objected, I suppose, when you decided to replace father's name with yours on the company. Oh, everyone said I should. Lawyers, bankers. Why, the Stewart Company is a tradition, everyone said: it's always been the Stewart Company. I realized that it wasn't that important to me, but it seemed important to you . . . I let it happen . . . I feel the same way about your women."

Slater said, "What is important to you?"

"Father was. The Burr Company is. Having a child was, when we were involved in that . . . There are certain things I wasn't made for, I suspect. I couldn't carry a child beyond the third month, and I was never taken with bed . . . I suppose I live day-to-day, Slater. I like to work, and I'm not displeased with our life, except during these analyses of it."

"Carrie," Slater said, "I want a divorce. I want to marry Jen."

"When we were young," she said, "you came to me with the idea of changing your name from Francis to Slater."

"Slater was my middle name," he said. "A lot of men take their middle name."

"All right, but let me finish . . . At the time, I thought it was a silly notion. You were very intent on it, though, remember?"

"Francis is a hell of a name for a man!"

"I don't think it would have bothered a *man*. But you were a boy, really, twenty-four, twenty-five . . . a boy. I thought at the time what a lot of trouble it would be— changing it on the checking account, legal papers, so forth . . . to say nothing of getting people used to it . . . Well, it wasn't going to be trouble for me. I said to go ahead, if you wanted to, and you did. It worked out fine. I don't think anyone in Cayuta calls you Francis now."

"What has this got to do with a divorce, Carrie?"

"My yardstick has always been how much trouble it would cause me. A divorce would upset my whole life, Slater, and I don't want one."

Slater said, "Do you know I could kill you right now? I could honest-to-God kill you."

"No, Slater, that's something you can't make yourself believe just because you say the words. You're letting off hot air, that's all. Most of this discussion is; most discussions are."

"You wouldn't know anything about hot, Carrie."

"I know about you. I know a little about hot, too. I know that hot doesn't stop and figure things out, as you do. Hot—love—whatever you want to call it, takes what it wants. There's nothing to stop hot from running off with a Jennifer McKenzie, anytime he's ready. Oh, he'd have to give up a lot, but isn't hot, love—whatever you want to call it—irrational? . . . Hot takes what it wants, and it keeps what it wants, Slater. I know a little about it. I don't go in for labelling things, but I know about things, a whole lot more than you do . . . Now, take me home, and bring the Cloward boy. He's too drunk to drive."

"I'll take you home, all right!" He was shaking with fury, shaking and holding himself back from simply walking over and knocking her backward, down into the highway, a drop that was far enough to kill anyone . . . even Carrie, hard and tough as she was.

"And bring the Cloward boy."

"The hell with the Cloward boy!"

"He could be you, Slater, years ago."

"Meaning what, Carrie?"

"Meaning stop hiding behind words. You were the same kind of kid he is . . . wide-eyed at the rich, always with the comb in your back pocket ready to preen, dreaming of driving the kind of car you're driving tonight, chasing after some maverick daughter of a rich man, calling it love . . . and then fourteen years later, surprised that it all didn't turn out like Paramount Pictures . . . surprised that there's responsibility attached, and then you can't just walk out as easily as you walked in!"

"Goddam you, Carrie," Slater said, "Goddam you! . . . I loved you when I married you. I was in love with you!"

"Get the car, Slater, and bring him," she said. "I'll wait here."

He crossed the gravel drive with the fury ready to snap his brain. As he went by the rows of parked cars, he heard the strains of "Hey, There," from the clubhouse, and he heard a voice singing lazily in the August night: ". . . love nev-ver made a fool of you, you used to be soooo wise, you—"

He stopped by Kenneth Leydecker's Chrysler. Behind the wheel was the Cloward boy, his head leaning against the window, his mouth hanging open, singing foolishly. The key was on in the ignition, with it, the car lights.

Slater reached across the boy and turned off the key, the lights.

"Thank you very much, old bird, but I better be moving along, Mr. Leydecker, sir, old bird."

"C'mon Cloward! Ass!"

"Hey there, you with your nose in the air, love—" the boy sang; he was too drunk to understand anything.

Slater put his hands on his shoulders and pulled him from the car. He walked him across to the Jaguar, put him in the front seat.

He turned on his headlights when he got in on the other side. Straight ahead, on the bank, the pink-and-white dotted chiffon showed in the moonlight, the long white arm, the incongruous leather strap of her wrist watch. Beside him in the Jaguar, the Cloward boy leaned into him, kept up his intoxicated singing, stopping and starting up again, his words thick and slurred, head dangling.

"Just shut up!" Slater yelled. His anger at Carrie was wild in his voice, and he wished now that he had gone back into the clubhouse to tell Jen good night, to tell her he would work something out; he wouldn't lose her. He imagined her waiting for him, watching through the crowds for him, wondering where he was.

He felt like just scaring the hell out of Carrie, roaring the Jag up with a near miss, so she would have to jump out of the way. He gunned the motor forward, headed right for her, and in the slow second before he swung to avoid hitting her, he imagined her jumping back and falling down the bank to the highway, a straight-line drop-off. The sudden thud of Carrie's body against his grill amazed him. He slammed on the brakes and jumped out. The chiffon was already soaking with blood, and Carrie's face—the eyes lusterless like those of a fish at the end of a hook—stared up at him.

He did not touch her, but instead, began to run. He ran up the side yard, for some reason toward the lights of the club kitchen, acting on a stupid impulse to get water, to wash out the blood, wipe away the incident . . . just clean it all away. Then he stumbled and fell to his knees, and in the darkness on his knees, he could hear someone shouting.

"It's Mrs. Burr!"

He pulled himself to his feet.

"Oh, Jesus Christ, she was run over! She isn't moving."

This time he began running back toward the Jaguar, as though he had not been anywhere near it . . . as though he were running from the clubhouse.

He saw two men standing by his car, pulling the Cloward boy from behind the wheel where he had slumped when Slater had jumped out.

nine

The door of the Men's in Walsh's Place opened and closed, and Slater Burr looked across at Cloward.

"I'm sorry to barge in on you," said Cloward, "but I wanted to talk with you. I called you last night around eleven, and three or four times today."

"How are you, Buzzy?"

"I don't go by that name much, any more, Mr. Burr. Donald."

"You wanted to talk to me?"

"Yes . . . It's not a very pleasant subject, and I'm sorry for that, on Christmas Day."

"Well?"

"And thank you for the Christmas card. For all of them."

"All right."

"I wanted to talk to you about—the accident that night."

"I should think you'd want to forget it. I've forgotten it," said Slater, "and I should think you'd want to . . . Are you out of Brinkenhoff for good now?"

"They don't give vacations, Mr. Burr . . . Yes, I'm out."

"I'm glad of it, Donald. It was very unfortunate—the whole thing. If you don't mind," and he started the motions of leaving, "I'd like to keep it forgotten."

Cloward touched the sleeve of his jacket. "Wait! Listen a minute. I've had a lot of time to think about that night, to go over everything, Mr. Burr."

"And?"

"Every time I went over it, one thing stuck in my mind. One thing. Someone moved me, Mr. Burr. I was sitting in Leydecker's car, and someone moved me."

"Donald, at the time, you said Leydecker gave you the keys to his car. You said you must have just wandered over to mine afterwards. Leydecker denied giving you the keys, and you didn't have his keys when you were found in my car . . . I think it's all best forgotten."

Cloward said, "Please listen to me, Mr. Burr . . . I know he gave me the keys. I know I was in his car, last I remember."

"Why do you want to go over and over it, Donald? It doesn't change your position any." Slater started toward the door. "Forget it!"

"In *your* eyes, it would, Mr. Burr. What if you knew that Leydecker put me in your car, sir? What if you knew that Kenneth Leydecker put me in your Jaguar, not so I'd run down Mrs. Burr, but so I'd run off the bank your car was facing! Mr. Burr, I couldn't have seen that sharp turn, drunk as I was! I would have gone straight down to the highway. I almost did, didn't I?"

Slater Burr's hand dropped from the doorknob. He turned around and looked at Donald Cloward.

Cloward said, "I want you to know I didn't steal your car. I never would have—not your car . . . For whatever reason he had, sir, Kenneth Leydecker put me in your car. I know damn well he did!"

ten

After Donald Cloward followed Slater Burr into the Men's, Chris and Lena McKenzie began dancing. Jitz Walsh started a conversation with Jen Burr about his European travels during the war, and Mona Sontag carried her beer down to the other end of the bar, rejoining her date.

"Welcome back," said Albert Secora, "or are you just slumming for a few minutes?"

"I was having a very nice conversation with the doctor."

"The doctor! If he's a doctor, I'm an astronaut."

"A veterinarian is a doctor, Al." She pronounced it vet-ah-naran. "Maybe not an M.D. but . . ."

"A V.D. maybe, Mona?" Secora guffawed at his little joke. "Yeah, a V.D. . . . in charge of syph and gon. And I'm an astronaut . . . Hey, did you hear the joke about the astronaut?" She was watching the McKenzies dance, and he had to poke her arm to get her attention. She looked down at her sleeve and his fingers there, as though a garbage man had his hands on her. It infuriated him, but he went right on with what he was saying.

"Hey, Mona? Knock. Knock."

"All right!," she said tiredly. "Who's there?"

"Astronaut."

"Astronaut who," she said in a bored voice.

"Astronaut what your country can do for you, but what you can do for your country!" He gave a loud snort. Mona merely sighed peevishly. She said, "I don't think it's nice to make fun of the President of The United States of America."

"Oh, for Pete's sake!"

"Well, it isn't. You just don't have respect."

"You don't mean for the President, you mean for Slater Burr."

"I heard you talking to him, Albert, all about how good the old days were, when Mr. Stewart was running the place."

"So what?"

"He knew what you were getting at. He moved away from you, didn't he?"

"What the heck do I care what he does, for Pete's sake! You know how long I'll be working for him, when G.E. gets here—about two seconds."

Mona Sontag said, "When I go out with someone on Christmas Day, the very most important day in the year practically, I expect the certain someone to behave like a grown-up man! . . . Did I whine around about work? Big people don't like it, Albert. They come in to relax like anybody else, and they don't like their employees sitting around griping."

"*Big* people! Oh, wow! *Big* people!"

"Well, he owns the place where we work, doesn't he? Lock, stock and barrel!"

"I suppose it's all right for you to sit up there and get free medical advice from that horse doctor, though, ha, Mona?"

"A man enjoys discussing his work. I was having a very nice conversation with the doctor."

"Well, I was discussing Slater Burr's work, wasn't I?"

"He knew what you were getting at. He moved away from you, didn't he? He went off and danced with his wife!"

"Was he supposed to ask me for a dance, Mona?"

"He did it to get away from you."

"Heck with it!"

He sipped his beer silently for awhile; then Mona got around to the subject she was dying to talk about. She waited long enough for the edge to be off their testy conversation, and she said, in a conciliatory tone: "What I wonder, is what's going on in the Men's right now."

"Same thing going on in the Women's, Mona, only in one place they're standing up, and in the other they're sitting down."

Secora wondered too, but he was still smarting at her words.

"On Christmas Day . . . of all the disgusting remarks . . . And that's another thing, Albert, that's another thing. Did you notice that I paid absolutely no attention to the drama taking place down at this end of the bar? I paid no attention, just went right on with my conversation with the doctor."

"If you weren't paying attention, how did you know there was a drama taking place?"

"What I mean, Albert, is that I didn't gawk at them."

"Aren't you wonderful, though!"

"You gawked! Gawked right up at them! . . . I was just as

surprised as you were to see Donald Cloward walk in here, but I paid no attention."

"I bet you don't perspire, either, Mona. I bet you don't ever have to blow your nose, or clean under your nails, or any of the things we human beings indulge in, ha, Mona?"

"I don't gawk!"

"Well, Merry Christmas, Mona. You can just bet your neck that I'm delighted I socked ten ninety-eight into that brooch I gave you!"

"You want it back, Albert?"

"Heck with it! *Big* people! . . . I could tell you a few things about Mr. Big in the can there! If he's so big, why doesn't he have the price for a motel when he wants to make out, or a hotel even!"

"Referring to what exactly?"

"Referring," Albert Secora said, "to a night I saw him up at Blood Neck, in his car, with Jen Burr, before she was Jen Burr!"

"You kidding me? They didn't even give each other the time of day, until his wife was killed."

"Heck they didn't. Me and a certain party, who shall remain nameless, as she is married to someone else, saw them up there. Parking. Couple of months after she first hit town."

Mona Sontag shoved her beer glass forward on the bar top to signal a refill. She said, "Honest to God?"

"Honest to God . . . Now, if he's such a Mr. Big, Mona, why didn't he hire a motel, or even a hotel? He was up there same as I was, and for the same reason."

"You sure?"

"Just as sure as I am that he kept me on the payroll three months while I was sick, so I wouldn't mouth it around!"

"What do you mean, Albert?"

"Well, I had an accident next day. I had a fall and broke some ribs. You think he'd a kept me on three months, unless he had a good reason? He didn't want me mouthing around what I saw."

"G'wan!"

"You don't remember the time I was sick three months?"

"I never paid any attention to you. I was engaged to be married to Wally Herman at the time."

"Well, he kept me on, so's I wouldn't mouth it around."

"I bet you did anyway."

"Naw, hell, whatta I care what he does! He was laying Mitzi Caxton once, years and years back too!"

Jitz Walsh walked back and took Mona Sontag's glass, put it under the beer jet; then refilled Secora's too.

"There's a lot of things goes on in this town," said Secora. "For instance that high-and-mighty wife of the so-called doctor. She used to hang around up to Farley's Lake with Jitz here. Years before Chris McKenzie moved to Cayuta."

"Oh, I know that."

"She acts like she never seen him before now. I was noticing when she come in. 'Hello, Lena,' he says, and she says, 'Ha-lo, there,' real snippy like. Ha-lo there . . . like she never even heard of Farley's Lake."

"Well, I never heard that Slater Burr was hanging around with Jen McKenzie before they were married."

"Oh, yeah . . . Yeah, I was floored and so was Francie, when we saw them drive in at Blood Neck."

"Not Francie Boyson."

"We used to get together, time to time."

"Rich Boyson's fat slob of a wife?"

"Eight years ago she was fat in the right places."

"God, Francie Boyson! I should think anyone could do better than that!"

"She suits him, don't she? Suits Rich, and he owns his own place, which is more than anyone you go out with owns!"

"Including you."

Secora was going to answer her, but then the door of the Men's opened, and out came Slater Burr and Donald Cloward. Burr had his arm around Cloward's shoulders.

Beside Secora, Mona sucked in her breath.

Secora said, "Well, well, well, lookit that. They're old buddies all of a sudden."

"Don't you start anything, Al."

"Start anything? What the heck am I going to start, for Pete's sake?"

"Well, don't gawk and butt in. You know."

"I do *not* know! What am I? Some kind of a horse's ass? I know how to conduct myself, same as you."

"It's your hostile attitude I worry about. You know what hostile means?"

"No, Miss Webster's Dictionary and Encyclopedia, I'm stupid or something, for Pete's sake!"

"Just be nice, Albert."

"I am nice! You don't give me credit for knowing the alphabet!"

Slater Burr led Cloward to the bar. "Hey, Jitz!" he called out. "Let's set 'em up here, fellow . . . What're you drinking, Buzzy?"

eleven

The night Jen told Chris McKenzie she was marrying Slater Burr, they had this conversation:

"I can't say I'm happy, Jen."

"I'm not asking you to be, but you could hope that I'll be happy."

"You're 22, and he's 40."

"39."

"All right, 39. It's the same thing."

"What do you have against him, besides the fact we were having an affair before Carrie was killed?"

"Nothing against him, Jen. It's just that you don't know what you're getting into. He's more complicated than you know. Carrie Burr was complicated too. They suited one another."

"She never liked the same things Slater did, never."

"But she knew what he liked and let him have it. She knew how to manage him. She knew him like a book. You don't."

Jen had laughed. "She didn't know Slater at all, not at all."

"Don't be foolish, Jen. They were married 14 years. What I mean is, she kept him jumping."

"You make him sound like a little dog who jumps through a hoop for his trainer."

"Maybe that's the way it was. Don't be so sure you can make him happy. He's a grown man, and you're a child in more ways than age."

"You think I'll bore him?"

"It's possible you'll bore each other after awhile."

"And then, Chris?"

"I don't know," he had answered.

Now he knew. Night after night, drinking as they did, he knew.

Others in Cayuta knew as well as Chris knew. Only last week when Elmo Caxton brought his dog in with Harder's gland, the subject had come up.

"How's your sister"—Caxton.

"Well, I hope she's all right," Chris had said.

"They seem to get out a lot, seem very lively," Claxton had remarked.

"Slater Burr does too much drinking," Chris had told Caxton. "It worries me. He doesn't worry me, but my sister could just as easily go the way I did."

"Runs in families, does it?"

"Well, now, I'm not saying that. No, that's not a fact, but . . ."

"Pretty thing like her. Too bad," Caxton had ended the conversation.

No, it wasn't just Chris who knew, never mind Lena's complaint that Chris was obsessed with the subject of alcoholism. Give Lena enough rope and . . . well, look at her right now, Chris thought as he stood in Walsh's Place. She had gone past her limit three beers ago. She was down by the jukebox, performing a little dance solo, her glass in her hand, singing softly to herself.

It was Slater, though, who irritated Chris the most. He was very high, encouraging Cloward to elaborate on his flimsy theory of what had happened the night Carrie was killed. Everyone in Walsh's Place was listening; by now, making no pretense of it, even joining in—the way Secora was, agreeing with all of it, and telling Slater everything Slater said was right. Jen was very intoxicated too, mothering Cloward, smoothing his hair and calling him "poor baby" (both of them, not a year apart in age) and Miss Sontag was watching the proceedings through bleary, half-shut eyes, saying over and over, "I ought to report Mr. Leydecker to Father Gianonni. He's a priest; he'd know what to do."

Slater, of course, was buying the drinks.

" 'Nother round," Slater told Jitz, ". . . and he actually said he hated you, Buzzy?"

"He said he loathed me," Cloward answered.

"Said it right out, ah?"

"That's why I got so drunk, I think. I was upset. I'd never been to the club, never been out with him and Laura that way."

"And he gave you the keys, drunk as you were?"

"Yes. Laura had gone on. Mr. McKenzie here—he took Laura home. She was sick, something was wrong with her ankle." Cloward looked at Chris for confirmation. Chris shrugged his assent. He remembered taking Laura Leydecker home, remembered her complaint that she had synovitis of the ankle. He remembered too that Leydecker had seemed almost eager for his daughter to drive with them; he had wanted to stay on, which was peculiar enough, for a man who rarely went to the club, whose friends never went there. Maybe Leydecker had said all the things Cloward claimed, and maybe he did give Cloward his keys, and hope Cloward would kill himself. What did it change? Cloward still wound up behind the wheel of Slater's Jaguar, no matter the circumstances; it was still manslaughter, clear cut . . . And if it made Leydecker look bad, it did not make him a murderer now, nor even an accessory. Water over the dam; that was what most drunken conversation concerned itself with. Try to tell that to a drunk.

Still, it was wrong of Slater to encourage this sort of talk in public; it was the sort of vulgar shenanigans all drunks became involved in, and were sorry for the next day.

Chris said, "Slater, we really ought to push along."

"Go ahead. They out of ginger ale or something? Jitz? You out of ginger ale?"

Secora laughed hardily at the remark, and clapped his hand on Slater's shoulder. "You're a beaut, Mr. Burr!"

"Slater," Chris tried again, "we came in your car."

"Well, take the bus back, Carrie Nation. Buzzy, here, came out on the bus. Came looking for me. Clear his name. Like any man!"

Jitz Walsh set up another round of drinks, another ginger ale for Chris. Lena was sitting down in a chair now, near the jukebox, cooing to herself. Chris left her drink on the bar.

"I know Leydecker personally!" Secora said. "He's always butting into union meetings. I know him personally! Always blabbing about new industry. What the hell we need it for? We got The Cayuta Macaroni Company and Burr Manufacturing, ha, Mr. Burr? Shoe plant, and whatthehell!"

"That's right, Secora," said Slater. He put his hands on Cloward's lapels. "Buzzy here'd like to work for me. He's got an offer in New York working for a newspaperman, but he'd rather work for me."

"I feel lost in New York," said Cloward. "I dunno. The fellow I'm supposed to work for is carrying the torch for some girl. I get tired of hearing it. This is my home, here."

"Sure," Slater said. "And if what you say is true, if Leydecker put you in my car, well, now, hell! Hell, you got a gripe coming!"

Jen said, "I don't think you even ran into her. I think she jumped in front of . . ."

Slater cut her off. "Oh now, Jen. Crap! Jen! People knew Carrie better 'n that."

"Well, Slater, I . . ."

"The important thing is that Leydecker was out to get Buzzy! Now, I personally believe Buzzy! I think Leydecker did put him in my car. My car was pointed right at the drop-off."

Secora said, "Leydecker coulda pulled off the emergency and started the car rolling even."

"No," Cloward shook his head. "I hit her too hard. She could have jumped out of the way, Al, if I'd been rolling."

"Maybe she didn't want to jump out of the way," said Jen.

"Oh, now, Jenny! Now nobody gets killed with a car coming at them on a slow roll. Now, hell, you don't know anything about it! Why, at the time you were so daffy over Horace Dryden you couldn't see your nose on your face." Slater laughed and tickled her under the chin. "Good old Horace!" he said. "Fell in love with him when you saw the back of his neck! You all know that? Old Horace the Bore-ass was Jen's big moment that summer. Up at Blood Neck Point with him till the roosters crowed."

"Slater! Oh, Slater," and Jen laughed then. She sang, "I must have that doggie in the win-dow, the one . . ."

"With the fleas in his hair," sang Slater.

Secora let out another whoop of delight at Slater, and said, "Why shore, shore enough, old Blood Neck!" He feigned a playful sock at Slater's jaw. Slater looked uncomfortable. He downed his whiskey, while Secora turned to Mona Sontag and said, "How'm I doing? Am I nice or hows-stile?"

"I'm tired, Albert."

"Well, now, just when I'm having me some fun, you're tired."

"I can't help it . . . all this beer."

"Heck, Mona, it's Christmas Day!"

"I was going to church this evening."

Donald Cloward leaned into Slater. "I didn't come back to make trouble for Laura's father, Mr. Burr. I just want a start. I can't see myself in New York City."

"Sure, well, we'll talk about it," Slater said.

Mona Sontag murmured: "I ought to tell Father Gianonni about Mr. Leydecker. A priest knows what to do."

"Be funny," said Secora, "if Leydecker was driving the Jag himself."

Cloward said, "That wouldn't make much sense, Al. I don't think he'd just take Mr. Burr's car. He was nowhere near there either."

"He coulda run for it, left you there. Why wouldn't he, if he wanted you out of the way?"

"I don't think so . . . No," said Cloward.

Slater Burr said, "Secora, why don't you take Miss Sontag home? She's had it!"

Secora ignored the remark. "D'yah drive a Jag a lot, Buzzy, 'fore that night?"

"It was my first and last time."

"The one and only time, for Pete's sake? Heck, they're a little complicated. I don't think a drunk could figure it out, never been in one. Not figure it out and get all that speed up for a short distance . . . Now, I, myself, once drove a Jag. S'got an English shift, you know, more forward speeds than ours. I had to sit there awhile and figure it out, and I was dead sober."

"Any bright person could figure it out in a second, Secora," said Slater. "You better take Miss Sontag home, Mister. She's falling asleep."

"I ain't bright, or something?"

"I didn't say that . . . I just think you'd better take her home."

"I think I just did it instinctively," Cloward said.

"A Jag? It isn't like our cars, not the '54 ones. Course some of them are now. I'm talking about the old ones, Mr. Burr. I had trouble the day I tried one, was nine, maybe ten years ago."

"Tired, Albert," said Mona Sontag.

"She'll get a second wind," Secora told everyone. He turned back to Donald Cloward. "You didn't even have a trial, did you?"

"No . . . But . . ." Cloward was frowning.

Slater Burr said, "Take her home, Secora!"

"What's the matter with you, Mr. Burr? Leydecker could have been driving your car, couldn't he? Keys were left in it, weren't they?"

"Right now," said Slater, "I'm thinking of Miss Sontag. A gentleman takes a lady home when she's had enough!"

"Sla-ter," Jen touched his arm, spoke softly. "Not so rough . . . Go a little easy, darling."

"Thank you ver-ree much, Mr. Burr," said Mona Sontag. "He isn't gentleman."

"The heck I'm not! I spent ten ninety-eight on a . . ."

Slater had him by the arm now, and was taking him to the door of Walsh's Place. Chris McKenzie got off his stool and helped Mona Sontag.

"He isn't gentleman," Mona Sontag said.

"You don't have any right to do this to me, Mr. Burr!" Secora said.

"You horned in on the little party, now horn out!" Slater answered. He gave him a shove out the door, and Mona Sontag caught his arm and dragged along with him.

For a moment, the pair stopped in the drive outside Walsh's Place, and Chris McKenzie could see Secora's face, red and angry.

"You were pretty rough on him, Slater," Jen said.

McKenzie watched while the pair got into Secora's old Chevrolet. "They're all right now. They're leaving," he said. "We ought to go too."

"One on the house first," Jitz Walsh smiled.

"Well, not for Lena," said Chris. Lena could not drink any more if Walsh had taken one across to her. She was sitting down by the jukebox with her head on the table.

"You're a fine one, you are," Jen giggled, "talking about taking ladies home. Look at Lena."

"Lena didn't ask to go home," said Slater. He turned to Donald Cloward. "Secora was butting in. This sort of discussion shouldn't be open to public debate in a barroom."

A fine time to think of that, Chris McKenzie told himself.

Carrie Burr had never laughed much, but when she had, the laughter burst like an explosion—*whoom!* Slater could hear them in his mind, one after the other now, while he faced Cloward in his living room.

"No kidding, Mr. Burr," said Cloward, "I never thought of it before. Not until Secora said it."

"Secora is a know-nothing, Buzzy!" . . . All right, and there went another; oh, a know-nothing, is he, ummm, Slater, and ha! ha! ha! Whoom! Whoom! Whoom!

Jen said, "He's not our favorite person. He's one of the union leaders at the plant, Donald. I was surprised to hear him speak out against Leydecker that way. Leydecker's very thick with those union people, isn't he, darling? He's always speaking up for them at B.B.B.C. meetings."

"B.B.B.C.?"

"Buy, Build, Boost Cayuta," said Slater. "This is a hell of a town to want to settle in right now, Buzzy. Whole place is on the skids."

You are, you mean—Whoom! . . . But Slater smiled, relaxed looking, legs stretched out, big and easy-going, "Yeah, Secora talks through his hat! His kind tilts the way the wind blows, and the wind was blowing in the direction of free drinks this afternoon."

Cloward's short, freckled hands were playing with a comb, running their nails through its teeth and twanging them; his eyes slightly glazed from drink. "Still," he said, "I never thought of the fact I'd never driven a Jag before."

"It is interesting," Jen said.

"Jen, get dinner!"

"What?"

"I'm sorry," said Slater. "I'm just hungry. We all are."

"O-kay, but watch your tone of voice, or the cook will quit."

He watched her walk across the room toward the kitchen. And if she were to know the truth, what would she say or do? He knew what Carrie would have done under the same circumstances; she would have turned him in, graciously, of course, and emphatically; Carrie had been a woman of Character. But Jen? Ah, and he laughed inside, he knew. "We can hide out in Europe, Slater." It would represent another chance to get abroad . . . Maybe not. It was hard to know anyone any more, hard to know himself, and why it was he could sit there facing Cloward after Cloward's eight years in prison, and think only of two things about him: that he wished to God Cloward would put his comb away, and that he would have to get Cloward out of Cayuta, and fast.

It had all gone too far. In the beginning, Slater had thought it might be amusing—even useful—to have Cloward's theory on Leydecker's involvement in the accident go the gossip rounds in Cayuta. The idea of Leydecker thinking his daughter was too good for an honest working man would turn a lot of people of Secora's ilk against Leydecker . . . and it would sift through, reach others too. It would also renew everyone's interest in, and speculations about, Leydecker's daughter. That mystery had blown over in the past few years; eventually people simply accepted odd facts, the same as they accepted the fact that Horace Dryden's mother was a kleptomaniac, and Paul Ayres never touched money without wearing gloves, and Father Gianonni of St. Anthony's was a lush.

Slater had imagined some slight diversion from the idea of Kenneth Leydecker as the community's hope and rescuer . . . a little gossip to sidetrack the notion. He had even toyed, for the briefest moment, with hiring Cloward. To ease his conscience? No, he crossed that one off; he had gone beyond conscience a long time ago. In as far as he was now, he had become stout enough to throw off the chill of a bad conscience almost at once . . . But if he had hired Cloward, it would make him look as good as it made Leydecker look bad. An act of charity, forgiveness . . . It had seemed just that simple to Slater at Walsh's Place. Even though Cloward had not a shred of evidence against Leydecker in the manslaughter charge, it would start tongues wagging, that was all.

Then goddam punk Secora put his mouth in! There had not even been a suggestion that anyone could have been behind the wheel but Cloward, until Secora's dull brain sparked for the first time in his life.

Cloward sat opposite Slater in the Windsor chair, quite drunk now. They had all had a few more at Walsh's Place, before Lena fell on her face, and then they had mixed martinis here at home. In a way, Slater gave Cloward credit for picking up Secora's lead and not making anything out of it, but he did not like the fact Cloward dwelled on the matter, nor the fact Cloward wanted to stay in Cayuta. He was glad of this chance to straighten out his thinking and put it back on the wrong track.

Now Cloward was back on the subject of getting his newspaper friend interested in Secora's theory.

"Guy's real quick," Cloward was saying. "Things that take me all day to figure out, Guy figures out in seconds."

"What's he say to your theory of being put into my Jag by someone?"

"Well, you see, Mr. Burr, I never went into it too much with him. Guy used to say it was irrelevant. Irrevelant . . . because I still drove the car that killed her."

"He's right, Buzz."

"But if Leydecker were driving the Jaguar . . ."

"Wait a minute, Buzz . . . Now, listen to me."

"Yes, sir?"

"I personally hate Leydecker. He's causing me plenty of trouble. There's a new zoning law he's pushing and . . ."

"And he stole your father's ideas, or his father did. I remember my dad always saying that."

"Yes. Well, that's my point. There are a lot of reasons I don't like Leydecker. I'd be the first to want to prove what you say is true. Not just because I hate Leydecker, Buzz, but because, after all, my wife was killed in that accident."

"Yes, sir . . . I see."

"It's just a flimsy theory all the way around. You know Leydecker."

"Yes."

"He might give you his keys and hope you'd kill yourself, but as for Kenneth Leydecker taking a chance like that . . . Come on, use your head."

"Yes, I can see where it'd be unlikely."

"Leydecker wouldn't risk everything, and Buzz," Slater let out a small laugh, "he wouldn't have killed Carrie. He always liked Carrie! The whole idea is just bull, Buzz. Bull!"

"I guess you're right. It's far-fetched."

"You want to concentrate on your future, not your past."

"But you said yourself that Leydecker might very well have moved me to your car, sir. I wouldn't have taken your car, not yours!"

Slater said, "And that may be. And I believe you, Buzz. I think I believe you . . . But it doesn't help you now."

"Where you're concerned, it does."

"Yes. I'm ready to buy your theory, and it puts a different light on things, though I never felt angry at you. You were drunk. I've been drunk too."

"I'd really like to work for you, sir. I don't feel right in New York. I'd start anywhere, at any salary. I know it could be arranged . . . Sir, I don't want to be a secretary. What kind of a job is that for a man?"

"Okay," Slater said, "but wait a damn minute. It'll take time to arrange that through the parole board, right?"

"Right. It will take some time."

"And I've got to work out some problems . . . So why don't you go to New York, and work for this fellow for a time, and then I'll send for you."

"That would be just great, Mr. Burr!"

"I'd have to write your parole board and so forth."

"Yes, sir!"

"And in the meantime, I wouldn't shoot off my mouth to this newspaper fellow about your plans. You let me handle it."

"Don't worry, Mr. Burr."

"It might take a little time, but we'll do it, Buzz. Now, that's a promise."

"Thank you, Mr. Burr."

"And the sooner you go to New York, the better."

"Why is that, sir?"

"Well, if it looks as though you're back here to make trouble, Leydecker might get into it. He could write your parole board just as well. Gossip gets around. God knows what Secora is saying right now."

"I see what you mean . . . But I'm not supposed to leave until the end of the week."

"We might arrange it so you can leave earlier."

"Where would I go?"

"Hell, Buzzy, you been cooped up a long time! How about a hotel, money for some shows . . . have a little freedom. You won't get it around here."

Slater got up and walked across with the martini pitcher, poured Cloward another drink. A euphoria was rising in him now, dissolving the edge of panic he had felt earlier. No more whooms in his head; *I am getting away with it,*

Carrie, and he ruffled Buzzy's hair, "We'll work things out," and he began to feel all right again.

Buzzy Cloward said, "One thing, though . . ."

"What's that, Buzz?"

"Well, I keep wondering about Laura, about what happened to her."

II.

At ten o'clock, Kenneth Leydecker, his green celluloid eyeshade fixed to his brow, sat at his tambour desk in his study, rereading the speech he had composed for Thursday's meeting of the B.B.B.C., ". . . and to attract industry we must have lower rates of interest for financing it. The State of Pennsylvania will go as low as two per cent, whereas New York requires at least five and a half per cent. Furthermore . . ."

The ringing of the telephone surprised him. He looked at the telephone as though there had been some mistake, but on the second ring, he picked it up.

"Hello?"

"I would like to speak to Laura."

"Laura is in bed at this hour," he said.

He heard the click on the line, and knew that Laura was on the extension upstairs. He had known this call was inevitable, but he had not been prepared . . . now with Laura listening, he felt shaky and apprehensive.

Donald Cloward said, "It's only ten o'clock."

"Nevertheless, Laura is in bed."

"What's the matter with her, Mr. Leydecker? You know who this is."

"Yes, I do know who it is."

"I want to know what's the matter with Laura. Is she a prisoner or something?"

"I think that's your status, much more than it is Laura's."

"That was my status. Now I want to know Laura's!"

"She wants nothing to do with you, Donald."

"I'd like to hear her tell me that . . . I want to hear her tell me that she's all right."

"I'm afraid that's impossible."

"Why?"

"Why? Because it is!"

"I'm not trying to start anything up again, Mr. Leydecker. I'm going away soon, but I want to know if Laura's all right."

"She is all right. Now, there's nothing more to say, Cloward."

"I want to talk to her. When can I call her?"

"If you call here again, I'll call the police. Donald, I don't want you to bother us again!"

"I just want to talk to her! I've got to know if she's all right."

"You'll have to take my word for it."

"The same way I took your word about the car keys, Mr. Leydecker?"

Kenneth Leydecker dropped the phone into its receiver. He waited a moment, then picked it up again, and got a dial tone. He was relieved. Laura had hung up at the same time.

thirteen

In the car, Jen Burr tried to make him feel better about it.
"We've all done things like that, Don."

"I shouldn't have called there. I don't know what got into
me. I was sitting there by myself in the living room, and
suddenly I remembered her phone number. I just thought
I'd try seeing how she was."

"You get a good night's sleep, and everything will be all
right in the morning. You're still a little tipsy. Things always look worse."

It was something she told herself, as well as Cloward.

She had been left with no alternative but to drive Cloward
home. While Cloward was phoning Laura Leydecker in the
living room, she and Slater had been arguing in the kitchen.
It was her own fault for nagging Slater. She had begun with
a complaint about his remark at Walsh's Place, that she
had been to Blood Neck with Horace Dryden (lecherous
creep!), and it had ended with her telling Slater he was behaving like some sort of criminal, covering his tracks, lying,
then this new idea to spirit Donald off to New York City
tomorrow, unbeknownst to anyone.

She should have been perceptive enough to realize that
Cloward's return was dredging up all the mucky guilt and
self-recriminations Slater carried around inside him. Lord,
last night she had gotten a close enough look at it, Slater
slapping her that way. She should learn to leave it all alone,
let Slater work it out himself, however he chose to do it.

Slater had gone up to bed angry at her. Another First,
she thought sadly; last night a sock in the jaw, tonight going
to bed in a huff. They never had those kinds of quarrels,
never. There was not a thing in the world which could happen between them, that their bodies near each other could
not diminish in seconds . . . Yet tonight, she had gone into
the bedroom to get the keys to the car, leaned over Slater
and touched his shoulder: "I'm taking Donald home, darling."
. . . "Do as you please, darling," he had answered sarcasti-
cally . . . And for a horrible few moments as she went down

the stairs, she had the feeling he missed Carrie, and that Slater and she were all wrong together; why hadn't she known that all these years? Why hadn't she listened to Chris? He had warned her Slater was too complicated. Carrie knew how to handle him.

"I did everything wrong tonight," Donald Cloward said beside her.

"You're not the only one."

"Now I have Mr. Burr angry at me."

"He was angry at me, Donald. He's under a lot of pressure, and sometimes I forget that."

"I don't see why he didn't tell me good night. It's as though he knew I'd called Leydecker."

"No, he didn't know it. And I won't tell him tomorrow. It was a quarrel we had, in the kitchen. It didn't have anything to do with you."

But I'll be glad when you're gone, Jen thought . . . Maybe she and Slater ought to cut out the drinking; maybe Chris was right: it made good things bad, bad things worse. Sometimes Chris' corny clichés hit their mark. Ah, but God, not Slater and her, there wasn't anything wrong there. It was the goddam town and goddam Leydecker, and now the Cloward boy coming back like this. Still, she felt sorry for Donald Cloward. He had told her about his newspaper friend and the long hours spent listening to him pour out his troubles, while Donald sat feeling no one wanted to hear his, and that there was no one.

She said, "We've all had too much to drink."

"You certainly can hold it, Mrs. Burr."

"I shouldn't be driving. I can feel my drinks."

"I shouldn't have let you bring me home. I should have called a cab."

Jen said, "They take hours to get to our place."

"Or a bus, or something."

"A bus!" Jen laughed. "The buses don't run after five o'clock in Cayuta any more . . . . People either have cars, or they're too poor to go out."

"Yes, it's all changed . . . Buy, build, boost—Cayuta! But it feels like home, you know?"

"You're lucky to be leaving. I wish we were."

"I'll be back though. Unless Mr. Burr's mad at me now."

"He has no reason to be mad at you, Donald. Get it out of your head."

"I shouldn't have called Laura, but I wish I could just

see her. I don't love her. I don't think I love her. Maybe I never did. It's hard to say. But I'd like to know what's wrong, why she never comes out any more."

"Donald, you're driving me crazy with that noise you're making with the comb."

"I'm sorry." He put it back in his pocket. "It's a habit. I know it's irritating. I saw Mr. Burr look at me back at your place once. I was doing the same thing, and I could see in his eyes he was disgusted . . . I have to watch myself. I've been away so long, I'm not used to people. I forget . . . For awhile there, back at your place, I realized I was talking too much about—the other Mrs. Burr."

"What do you mean?"

"I was just saying how much I liked her. He acted sort of angry, you know what I mean? I realized it must have stirred up a lot of old memories for him. It must have hurt him. No offense, or anything, but it must have been hard for him to remember the other Mrs. Burr. I've got to watch myself."

"What did you think of her, Donald?"

"She was always swell. I mean, everyone liked her. Mr. Burr worshipped her, I guess. I shouldn't have brought up her name so much."

"Don't feel guilty about it, Donald. Maybe he doesn't like to think about her, but it wasn't all the way you thought."

"I guess I shouldn't even be talking about it now. I'm too drunk . . . But I did like Mrs. Burr."

Jen felt a tiny dart of anger, just a sliver, enough to make herself say, "What was so great about her?"

"She was kind."

"Oh, kind . . . Sure. Just between you and me and the proverbial lamp-post, Donald, she was a bitch!"

"Of course, I didn't know her well, but . . ."

"Carrie Burr was far from kind. They were never happy, so just put your mind to rest on that score."

"I always thought they were."

"Everyone did," said Jen, turning on to Genesee Street. "But it wasn't so. If she hadn't been killed, Slater would have divorced her."

"Really, Mrs. Burr?"

"Really . . . It's bad enough to have her life on your conscience, but don't have their happy marriage on your conscience too. It just wasn't a happy marriage."

"Are you sure?"

"Yes, I'm sure, Donald . . . And I'm sure you didn't do

any harm calling the Leydeckers either. So sleep well tonight."

"You're great, Mrs. Burr. I mean, you understand what it's
like to feel—oh well, crummy."

"Yes, I know what it's like . . . Poor Slater, he's felt pretty
crummy for a long time, and I'm afraid I haven't been much
help."

"I think you're both wonderful people, Mrs. Burr!"

"Thanks . . . We like you too, Donald . . . Well, here we
are."

"I wonder if Mr. Leydecker will tell Laura I called?"

"The best thing is to forget all about the Leydeckers."

"I know that," he said. "It's just that I wonder about
Laura. I guess it's the drinks."

"It always is . . . No, you get a good night's sleep."

"Mr. Burr said I was to come out to your place tomorrow.
We'd figure things out."

"Then I'll see you tomorrow."

He got out of the car and then ducked his head inside for
a moment. "You've been just swell, Mrs. Burr!"

"Sweet dreams," said Jen.

"Thank you, ma'am."

He slammed the door shut and watched her car turn on
Capitol Street. Then he started towards the entranceway of
The Burr Building. He glanced at his wrist watch, pausing a
moment in the wet street, looking across at The Clark Building. After a second or more, he turned away from the entranceway, down Genesee, weaving a little from left to
right, but going rapidly.

fourteen

When she had been very young, when her mother was still alive, in the years and years before Buzzy Cloward, she used to sit around the back porch steps with Peony Stubbs and Betty Jean Means, solemnly debating a preference between losing her hearing, or going blind.

"I'd rather be deaf any old day of the week!" she would insist. "If I were to go blind, I'd wish I were dead!"

And Peony would declare that she would wish she were dead if she could not hear, and Betty Jean Means, stuck on horror stories of World War II, told by an older brother, would ask them both what they thought of being "basket cases." Wasn't that worse than going deaf or blind?

Laura Leydecker often thought of those days and that particular theme, when she went nightly down the back stairs to fix her snack before the 11:15 late show on television. She turned on as few lights as she could. There were no near neighbors on Highland Hill. Not near enough to see from their windows into the Leydeckers'. But the thought was always there that someone might look in, see her through the straw blinds in the kitchen, the same way she could see the outlines of the pine trees and hydrangea bushes outside. She crept around in an old robe of her father's; the wig made her flesh creep, she never wore it, someone else's hair, like someone's hand sewed on; no, let any busybodies think it was him raiding the icebox; him whom she hated . . . and she thought how much better it would have been, had blindness struck than this unimaginable thing. This Thing was somehow shameful, laughable, as she had always been laughable, really, oh, she knew that . . . but blind . . . Blind she could have gone to one of those schools for the sightless, entered their world and stayed among them . . . and she had fantasies of that being what had happened. Sometimes she would shut her eyes going up the back stairs and see how easy it was to maneuver . . . Or in her room, she would sometimes turn off the sound on the television set, watch it and think of being deaf.

Both alternatives were better. To be the way she was, was to be Betty Jean Means' "basket case." The irony of those discussions and those days (O how hysterically and gleefully she had laughed when her mother sang the song about the ball being over, and Mary taking out her false teeth, her false eye, taking off her wig!) was renewed nearly every day.

No amount of newspaper clips left under her door by her father, telling of wigs being The Fashion, could do war with the bitter fact she would rather die than let it be known. God, Fate was like Dreams the way it chose just the right thing for you, so brilliantly and cruelly selective in its choice . . . wouldn't you know *that* would happen to Laura Leydecker, ha ha's down the tunnel of her imagination, wouldn't you just know it would be something like *that!* . . . And in her bureau drawer, the gold-back brushes of her mother, and gold-edged combs to mock her.

She had tried; tried everything every doctor told her, and long after she had stopped seeing doctors, stopped mourning the loss of Buzzy, stopped everything but living in the world of her room, there was nothing to change things. Only in dreams was it any different, and that was nearly every night. The same, the same: the whole thing had simply never happened. There she was! Walking down Highland Hill, brown hair spilling to her shoulders, blowing ever so lightly in the breeze: *blown hair is sweet, over the mouth blown.*

Settling before the set again that night, at eleven-fifteen, she saw her reflection opposite the bed, in the mirror, while she ate the turkey, taken from the refrigerator downstairs. She looked to herself like some wild creature, gnawing a bone; and on purpose, she exaggerated her performance, contorting her features, ugly and crazy, all the while remembering the sound of his voice on the telephone an hour ago: *I want to hear her tell me that she's all right.*

Oh yes, fine.

"Really?"

"Yes, glorious, Buzzy!"

"Just as good as the last time?" he had murmured, his *mouth warm and moist at her ear. "Or better?"*

"The best and happiest moments of the happiest and best!"

"You say beautiful things all the time, don't you? Shakespeare and things."

"That was Shelley. You know it's usually Shelley. It was from his 'Defence of Poetry'."

"But those are words. I make you feel them, don't I?"

"Oh, yes! You do!"

It was hot that July afternoon, and he was very tan, his bronze-colored arms and legs and shoulders wet from love-making, but not heavy on her; he never once was. The lightest thing in the world was the loved one's body. He stayed that way smoking a cigarette, giving her a drag, touching the wetness of her hair at her forehead with his freckled fingers, kissing her gently at first and then with the renewed passion that was always there, the hard hanging-on of one to the other.

"Darling, do be careful. We have to dress. The man will be wondering what happened to us."

"I wonder if he'll keep this same crummy bed in here after we move in?"

" 'Bed of crimson joy, and dark secret love.' "

"Shelley."

"No, not that time. Blake."

"It's still a crummy bed."

"I love this place!"

And she had. She had closed her eyes in the few slow seconds of silence between them, and thought of memorizing it: this feeling of herself under him, the two of them wet and loving, so that there seemed to be no sensation but their joy. On the stairway as they left, she had said: "I think sometimes it's all an illusion. 'All is illusion till the morning bars, Slip from the levels of the Eastern Gate. Night is too young, O friend! day is too near!' . . . Don't you feel that way, darling?"

There was a tin guard loose on one step, the stairway dark, smelling of mustiness, coffee cooking, and the noise below of traffic in the street. She thought how beautiful it was that soon she would know every step of the stairs, every crack in the plaster, every detail of their home, and the sound of him on those steps coming up to number four at a day's end, waiting for that sound: how beautiful . . . And there was a roach running down the stairway, frightened and blind and ugly looking, and he had stepped over it, not wanting to kill it; that was him.

"I only worry about your father," he had said.

She put aside her plate of food and leaned back against the pillows. She closed her eyes and tried to remember what it had felt like, but her mind fastened on the bizarreness of herself under any man now. She opened her eyes. On the television screen a woman in tights, carrying a fan, was performing a seductive dance before a man sitting at a table, holding a drink, leering at her.

The woman was singing:

> "Do you know what it means?
> To miss New Orleans,
> When that's where you left your heart?"

She remembered an afternoon years back at Cayuta Lake, when a boy named Ted Chayka had looked that way at her. Chayka had gone to Industrial High with Buzzy; he was a big unruly fellow who fished off the pier at the lake and drank beer out of cans, always eyeing the girls who came to swim there. Buzzy had told him to stop staring at Laura; there had been a fist fight, and Buzzy had cut his eye. At home later, Laura had fixed a bandage to the cut, and her father had walked in the kitchen then, home from work. He had been unmoved by the story. As though Buzzy were not present, he had said, "If you'd been at the pier with a decent boy to begin with, Chayka wouldn't have bothered you at all. You were with someone of his own class. That was the reason you were treated in such a manner!"

Bed of crimson joy, and dark secret love.

She remembered . . . . an afternoon in summer, at the clearing in Hunter's Woods, the shelf fungus they had broken off a tree to write their names on, beside them on the ground; the lavender joe-pye weed near the spot Buzzy had lain his shirt, and the red-start warbling above them in the catalpa tree, while Buzzy undid the buttons of her blouse. And their eyes! The way they were looking at one another then, looking right into one another, as though eyes could touch the parts of a person, burrow right into the heart and hold it securely; keep it that way forever, in one long look like that, and then . . .

Laura Leydecker sat up in bed suddenly. She reached for the control panel of the television. She shut off the sound, listening. She heard the noise on her window pane, as though someone were throwing pebbles at it from down on the ground. Quickly, she turned off the set, and pulled the lamp chain. She sat in the darkness.

Again.

She stole out of bed and crept across, pulling up a slat of the Venetian blind.

By the light of the street lamp in front of the Leydecker home, she saw him.

He was standing beside the Engelmann's spruce, in the side yard. He was looking up at her window, and now, he reached down again, tossing a scattering more of gravel, some of it hitting the pane lightly, the rest, the wooden frame of the house.

Momentarily she watched, without moving, staying to the side of her window. Then, when he did it again, she reached out her hand, up under the blind, and raised the window a few inches. She got down on her knees, peeping out at him through the bottom slats of the blind.

She heard him call her name softly.

She was trembling now; again he called, "Laura? Laura?"

Her voice broke when she answered him. "Go away!" Her lips rubbed against the cold plastic slat, as she forced her words out, softly as she could manage.

"Laura, is it you?"

"Yes. Go away."

"I have to see you! I called your father tonight, but he wouldn't let me talk to you. I want to know if you're all right."

"Yes, but go away, please."

"Will you see me tomorrow?"

"I can't."

"Why? What's wrong with you, anyway?"

"I'm—ill."

"What's wrong?"

"It's . . . a form of alopecia."

"What? I can't hear you."

"I don't want to tell you. Please go."

"Can I come back tomorrow night?"

"No."

"Please! Let me come tomorrow night. I can be here any time you say, meet you down by the back porch, the way we used to. Please!"

"Go now, Buzzy!"

"Yes, you'll meet me tomorrow."

"Go now, or father will . . ."

"Tomorrow," he said, "nine-thirty tomorrow night. Okay?"

"Yes," she said. She began to feel weak and sick.

"I'll be here at nine-thirty!"

She waited long enough to be sure he had gone. She saw him walk away, saw his red hair under the street lamp, as he turned down Highland Hill, and then she sank back on her haunches and held her hand to her mouth, heaving up nothing but retching agony from deep inside.

II.

In the dream, Kenneth Leydecker was explaining the re-formulation of the zoning rules, at a luncheon. He was standing on the podium in the large dining room at The Mohawk Hotel, looking out at the faces of his audience, seeing now Paul Ayres, now Elmo Caxton, now . . . a light, a very bright light, just as he was stating the new boundaries, a glaring light suddenly . . . and then he was awake.

"Laura!" He jerked himself up, his eyes blinking, his hands fumbling for his glasses.

"Father, you have to go to Buzzy and talk to him."

"I have to do nothing of the kind, Laura! I certainly do not have to do anything of the kind . . . Now what's this all about?" adjusting his spectacles on his ears and nose. Her eyes were bloodshot and tearful, her mouth quivering. She stood bare-headed, wearing his old robe and her pajamas under it, barefoot . . . suddenly pathetic-looking, worse than he could remember, the defiance gone out of her. He had always hated the defiance, but now that it was replaced with this hopeless despair, he realized how much easier it had been for him the other way.

"Laura," he said, "I know you heard the telephone call."

"You have to see him, father. You have to go and see him. I want you to do that for me."

"What good would that do? What would it accomplish? Laura, put your mind at ease. He won't come here."

"He just left here, father."

"He did *what?*"

"He was outside my window just now."

"I'm going to call the police." Leydecker's hand reached across for the telephone. Her hand stopped his.

"Father, please listen to me. I beg you to listen to me. For once!"

"Well, Laura?"

"He'll come back again. He will, father, no matter if you call the police or not."

"Don't you worry. The police can take care of him."

"Father, don't you understand? I don't want him taken care of that way. Haven't you done enough to Buzzy?"

"I did nothing to Donald Cloward, Laura. He did it to himself."

"The same way I did it to myself, is that it, father?"

"Laura, please. *Please*, Laura! Do you think I enjoy seeing you this way? Laura, if I could do *anything*—anything to help you, don't you know that I'd do it?"

"Would you, father?"

"Certainly!"

"Will you go see Buzzy? Will you go and tell him that I have an illness? Just tell him that I have an illness, father. You don't have to be specific! You can think of something. Tell him I have an illness that has changed me, and that I'm embarrassed to see him, or talk to him on the telephone . . . Father, if you did it in a nice way, he'd believe you."

"Laura, Laura, the police would see to it that . . ."

She shouted, "I don't want the police to do it, father! *You* do it!"

Tears formed in Kenneth Leydecker's eyes. He took off his glasses and wiped at his eyes with his fingers. "If you want that . . . then . . ."

"I want it, father."

"Very well, but . . ."

"Will you do it tomorrow? Tomorrow morning?"

"He had no right to come here." Leydecker sighed. "No right at all."

"I'm asking you, father, *will you do it?*"

"I said I would . . . He actually *came* here?"

"I was sick after . . . sick right on the floor of my bedroom. I could hardly walk in here."

"He just left?"

"I told you, father, he was just here!"

"All right," said Leydecker. "All right. I'll take care of it. You'd better take a pill, Laura."

"I shall, father."

"Yes, take a pill. You need some sleep."

"I wonder if anyone in the world gets as much sleep as I do," she said, walking out the door.

The moment the door was shut behind her, Leydecker took the telephone to his lap. He dialed the three digits which would ring the police.

"Who was it?" Nancy said.

"I'm afraid I have to leave early," Ted Chayka answered, as he walked back into the living room. On the floor beside her chair there were half-a-dozen red-stained Kleenexes wadded up and tossed there. There was the acrid, sickly-sweet smell of Milday Nail Polish Remover. Nancy's lap was peppered with tiny red peelings, nail size. This was her habit at night, to peel off as many of the red shells as she could from her fingers; then finish the removal of her nail polish with a liquid, on those nails she could not peel . . . Christmas night was no exception. The tree was lit on the T.V. top, a testimony to the holidays, and there were tie boxes and jewelry boxes there—their gifts to one another, and strands of tinsel were draped around the ears of the T.V. indoor antenna, but it was still just another day. Chayka was due at work at eleven-thirty, an hour away, and Nancy was probably fussing over in her mind, whether to watch the late show featuring Tyrone Power, or the mystery movie.

"Early? How come?"

He said, "That was Rich Boyson on the phone. My cousin's down to his place with a bag on."

"So let him. What's it to you?"

"It's Christmas night," said Chayka, depressed at the dullness of his voice, and at the irony of his own unnecessary announcement: *it's Christmas night,* "Rich doesn't want it spoiled for the customers."

"Is your cousin the only one who celebrates the holidays by getting a bag on? What's Rich Boyson in business for anyway?"

But she was not arguing because she cared that he had to leave an hour early; Nancy was just running off at the mouth again, about nothing at all.

Chayka said, "I guess things are out of hand . . . . Anyway, I said I'd stop in."

"There's a play coming on at ten-thirty, so I'll watch that, I guess."

"I'm sorry," Chayka lied. "I have to go, though."

"So—go." with a shrug of her shoulder.

"Want a can of beer from the icebox, while I'm up?"

"No, I want one from the oven."

"No sense being nasty, Nancy."

"Come on, Ted, I was kidding, for God's sake. Kidding, s'all."

"I guess I'm jumpy. I'll get you a beer."

"I don't know what's wrong with you lately, Ted."

"I don't know either," he said. "Nerves, I guess."

But he knew very well what was wrong. He thought about it while he got Nancy her beer, and then while he dressed in his blue patrolman's uniform—his shoes polished to a high shine, the crease in his pants sharp, the new black hatband on his cap, clean . . . the shield polished. He thought about it while he drove his old Plymouth down to Boyson's.

What was wrong was that he had changed.

He had been married seven years to Nancy, and during those seven years, he had changed from a hoarse-voiced, shiftless, drunk-every-weekend garage mechanic, to a solemn and sober member of the Cayuta Police Department. He had become something, and becoming that, he had realized there was more to go. He wanted ultimately to be a Police Lieutenant, a detective . . . but not just that . . . He wanted to be a happy and respectable citizen, Someone, as well as Something. He wanted to love his wife and have her kids . . . and there was Nancy every night, same as always, same as seven years ago, slopping around in her bedroom slippers, peeling off her polish, dropping her Kleenexes and her stockings and her empty beer cans wherever she had a mind to—going at Life with all the zest of a "before ad" for Geritol.

To make matters worse, it was all gone between them, as bad now as it had been wonderful in their teens, when they could not even wait out a movie in the darkness of the theater—not even a good movie, because every fiber of their being demanded more than the hand-holding, the furtive, futile groping: More and Everything.

Now, whenever he mounted her, he felt a sick, sinking loss, a feeling that invariably lent him enough anger to compensate for the emotion of passion, and it was a violent thing between them, quick and thankless. She received no pleasure; she did not have to tell him that, and she never did, in words. They never spoke about it . . . But it was there—in their mutual embarrassment at love scenes on T.V., in the child they could not conceive, in her "kidding" and his "nerves", and in the indifferent way of the passage of their years of married life.

"It's Christmas night."

"So—go."

It could not continue; if it did, the seven years of studying and working and getting-and-taking advice . . . and succeeding, step-by-step going ahead, would all be for nothing. . . . . It was not Nancy's fault that he had changed (God knows the drunken nights she had tolerated before Chris McKenzie came into their life to change him!) but it was not his fault either, that now he wanted more and better. And the more he wanted it, the better he wanted it to be, the worse it became between them. For a month he been unable to touch her—even to touch her, to try. Gone, and in its wake, a zero.

As he parked the Plymouth before Boyson's, he heard himself, in his mind, telling Chris about it, asking Chris about it. Tomorrow morning, when he was off-duty, he would go for coffee with Chris, air it—the whole thing . . . or it would drive him crazy, drive him back to the bottom of the bottle, where he used to look for solutions. Where there were none.

Rich Boyson was hovering near the entranceway of the bar, waiting for Chayka.

"Hi, Ted," he said. "My golly, I'm sorry, but . . ."

"Don't be, Rich!" Chayka told him. "Where is he?"

"Down at the end. I don't like what he's saying. I got to protect my good customers."

"Dirty mouth?"

"That I could handle myself, Ted. He's throwing around some pretty big names, not saying very nice things either."

"Okay, Rich."

Chayka walked back carrying his cap, nodding to this one and that one, and to Vincent, the bartender. When he came to the last stool at the bar, he said, "Hello, Al."

"Well, well, well! Himself!"

"You here all alone tonight?"

"Mona don't hold her drinks any better than you used to. I took her home. We was up to Jitz's place, at the lake."

"How about drinking up, Al?"

"Wha for? . . . Listen, you heard the joke about the astronaut. Knock. Knock."

"You've had enough, fellow. I'll give you a lift home."

"I got my Chevy outside."

"You're a little bagged to drive, Cousin."

"Yeah, yeah, well—so arrest me."

"I'll give you a lift instead."

"Let me finish first. I got half a beer . . . I got news too. News that ought to interest a policeman."

"Some other time, hmmm?"

"I was out with your sponsor s'afternoon, Ted. Isn't that what you alcoholics call your wet nurse? Yep! Me and Mona was drinking up to Jitz's place with the horse doctor and his wife, and Slater Burr and his *current* wife . . . and—get this, Cousin . . . And Donald Cloward."

Chayka studied Al Secora's cloddish features with contempt. The empty eyes, dulled by alcohol, shot with red, the thick mouth edged with beer foam, the brown hair mussed and lacquered with hair oil. Secora seemed to personify what Chayka himself had been called years back: that dumb Polack. And Chayka knew, knew as well as he knew that Secora would spill on himself half the rest of his drink, that handled a few inches this side of Rough, Secora would start a fight.

"Give me a ginger ale, Vincent," he said, and then, to reassure Rich's bartender, "A fast one for the road. Then we have to shove off."

"Yeah, I was honored to be amongst the big people, s'afternoon, Cousin. And I put a few twos together, for a four. A Police Department four."

Vincent shoved a glass of ginger ale down the countertop, and Ted Chayka picked it up, picked up Secora's glass and beer bottle with it. "Let's sit at a booth, Al. You can tell me all about it."

"I'm not kidding, Ted. I may be gassed, but I'm telling the truth."

They sat down across from one another.

"What truth?" Ted asked.

"I figured out that Slater Burr killed Carrie Burr, that's what truth."

"Sure. And I'm Milton Berle."

"No, no, you listen to me, Cousin. I figured it out. Donald Cloward remembers being moved from Leydecker's car to Slater Burr's. Someone moved him. He remembers that. He thinks it was Leydecker!"

"Un huh . . . What else?" said Chayka tiredly.

"Well, Slater Burr went along with it. He went right along with it, Cousin, up to a point. He says, 'Sure, Donald, Leydecker was out to get you.' He went right along with it, up until *I* brought up the fact a Jaguar isn't all that easy to operate, if you're gassed and you never operated a Jag before."

"It all makes a lot of sense, Al. Now how about working on your beer."

"You listen to me, Police Department!"

"I'm all ears."

"I'm telling you that Donald Cloward never drove a Jag. If he'd pleaded innocent and had a trial, any lawyer woulda fixed on that little point. He nev-ver drove a Jag . . . . But that's about all Slater Burr ever did drive, and it was Slater Burr's Jag, and Slater wanted Carrie Burr out of the way, so he could marry the horse doctor's sister!"

"That's a hell of a stupid thing to say, and you know it, Al!"

"Oh, I know it, ha? Listen, I saw them together—Jen McKenzie and Slater Burr, couple months before Mrs. Burr was killed. They was up to Blood Neck making out, same night I was up there with Francie. 'Member? Whatta you think I was kept on the payroll for when my ribs was busted? So I wouldn't squawk! That's what for!"

"What if they were there? That doesn't prove he'd murder his wife, even if he were having an affair with Jen Burr then."

"It'd establish a motive, though . . . es-tab-lish a motive, as they say on the T.V."

Secora slopped beer down the front of his shirt, and Chayka was relieved to see there was only an inch left in the bottle.

Chayka said, "Why don't you just worry about yourself, Al?"

"Because *I* don't have anything to worry about! And I'm tired of being pushed around!"

"Who's pushing you around?"

"Slater Burr pushed me the hell out of Jitz's place! He knew I was getting wise."

"Oh, sure. He has a lot to fear from you."

"Well, doesn't he? You ever think how much weight I throw around with the unions down to his place?"

"You're going to announce to the unions that he's a murderer, is that it? Oh, that's going to fix Mr. Burr, that is."

"Just don't say he's got nothing to fear from me! He can

afford another strike like I can afford to lay that broad he murdered his wife to marry!"

"Al," said Chayka, "listen to me now. You got a bag on and you feel your oats. But tomorrow you're going to wake up and feel like a goddam ass, shooting your mouth off down here this way."

"Crap, I am!"

"You know how it always is, the next day."

"Do you? Any more? Since you become Jesus Christ?"

"Al," Chayka forced a smile, "let me take you home now. You're beat! You could use some sleep. Work day tomorrow, you know."

"Slave day."

"Sure, well, how about it? I'll drive you up to your place, and tomorrow you can pick up your car . . . You know what a drunken driving rap means? A couple hundred bucks, and no license for a few months. Where would you be then? . . . And you'll get picked up, Al. There are extra men out tonight looking for someone to arrest. End of the month. You know how it is."

"You lousy cops would arrest your mothers. You mother-arresting cops!" He guffawed at his joke and drained the bottle of beer.

"C'mon, Cousin."

"Okay, but tomorrow isn't going to change today, and my two plus two equals four."

"We can talk about it tomorrow."

"It was Cloward got me on to it. Cloward was up there spouting like a goddam whale . . . all about how he remembers being moved from Leydecker's car to the Jag."

"Sure," Chayka said, helping his cousin out of the booth, "we'll talk about it tomorrow."

"Don't worry," said Al Secora, "I'm going to do plenty of talking about it tomorrow."

After he dropped him off, Chayka drove toward the station. If there were any way he could simply rub out Secora's kind, like a man rubbing out a roach under his shoe, he would do it. He was very familiar with all the nuances of the dumb punk putting in his nine-to-five, and nothing else; then hanging around beered up and belligerent at men who contributed a lot more than screwing bolts on by the clock. It was the Secoras, whose only responsibility outside a day's work was to keep their flies zipped up in public and pay their taxes grudgingly, who sat around scorning The Rich. Without The Rich, they'd be back rubbing stones together for fire, but it never penetrated their thick brains that men of responsibility and industry made it possible for them to loaf away their lives.

That was how Ted Chayka saw it, and he knew all the nuances. The borrowed glory of being at Jitz's place with Slater Burr's crowd, the drunken resentment at the fact he was one of them then, but not one of them . . . then the building up of his wobbly ego, by tearing them down . . . All in the glorious haze of alcohol, where the possibility of Slater Burr murdering his first wife was every bit as probable as Al Secora being the new Sherlock Holmes.

And tomorrow, Al Secora would talk about it. That was what angered Chayka. It would create nasty gossip in Cayuta among Secora's kind, and it would spread. Because there were a lot of people jealous of the Burrs, blaming Slater Burr for Cayuta's ubiquitous business problems, blaming anyone big enough to put the blame on, the same as Nancy blamed the Burrs or the Ayres or the Leydeckers for anything from an early winter to a two-cent rise on butter.

Chayka parked his Plymouth in the lot behind the station and stepped over the mud puddles on his way to the door. When he had coffee with Chris tomorrow morning, he would tell him what Secora had been shouting around Boyson's . . . let Chris hear it from Ted first . . . let Chris know where Al Secora stood with Ted Chayka; cousins was the end of it, cousins was the only fact to their relationship . . . and damn that fact!

The loudspeaker on the wall beside the coatroom droned: "Calling Car 7, in the third district . . . at Genesee and Maple, automobile accident . . . at South Corner on . . ."

"Ted?"

Chayka turned around and faced the desk Lieutenant.

"Don't bother taking off your coat. I'm putting you at it a few minutes early tonight."

"Sure . . . What is it?"

"Do you know Donald Cloward?"

"Sure."

"You know what he looks like, I mean?"

"I went to school with him."

"Good. He's been up bothering old man Leydecker. We just got a call. Leydecker says he left on foot, ten minutes or so. Check Highland Hill, then follow down Genesee to

The Burr Building. He's probably somewhere along that route."

"Who's driving?"

"Leogrande," the Lieutenant said. "He's out front with the motor going. Waiting. He wasn't sure he could identify him."

"I can," said Chayka, heading for the main entrance, "I used to hang around with him. Heard he was back."

sixteen

He often dreamed of Carrie. He never remembered the dreams, but he would awaken as he did in the gray light of six that morning, and feel her presence like a heavy veil of gloom enveloping him. And at those times, he would turn his head and see Jen beside him in the bed, and a wonderous relief would sweep through him, and reality would seem like found money, a clean bill of health from the doctor, a thing he did not want to do that he discovered he did not have to do.

He sighed and smiled, rested his large hand on the soft silk gown covering her thigh. He lay there with his eyes open, listening to a wet winter snow dribble in the tin drain trough, outside the bedroom window.

Random remembrances of Carrie wandered uneasily and sketchily through his thoughts, and fixed, finally, on their honeymoon night up in the Adirondacks. Throughout dinner at the main lodge Carrie had indulged in her usual shop talk, as though the day were no different from any other, and afterwards, over brandy, when Slater leaned forward and said softly: "Let's go back to our cabin now. You know how I love you, don't you, Carrie?" She had looked across the table and answered, "I suppose we'd better get at it." Very seriously. Slater had laughed at her way of putting it: poor, solemn Carrie, but she seemed annoyed at his laughter. He had paid the check, and the walk back through the woods was slow and silent. He had known, from the stiffness of her embraces before their marriage, that it would require patience on his part; he had imagined she was shy and embarrassed beside him, as they went toward their cabin; he had thought ahead of ways to make it easier for her. On a pretense of checking over the car, he would spend time away from the cabin while she undressed. He had given instructions to the lodge to have a bottle of champagne on ice in the cabin. Little, predictable touches to facilitate their love-making.

Once inside, almost the moment Slater turned on the lights,

Carrie began to undress. She did it matter-of-factly, the cigarette dangling from her lips, chattering away about a rotation bolt on a roller as she folded her slip and hung up her dress, and then, naked, she turned to Slater, who had begun to undress as well.

She said, "I don't think I'll be much good at this sort of thing."

She sat on the bed waiting for him. Her body was white and beautiful, slender and tall and small-breasted, and at the same time that Slater felt desire mounting in him he felt some loss, as though a sun were bright but not warm, as though the intriguing mystery of Carrie was simply not there: she really was what she was, no more; nor pretended to be more: it had all been in his eyes.

Still, she had received him easily, not gratefully, nor excitedly, but naturally, and afterwards she had lit a cigarette and begun talking of other things again.

He had said, "Did you feel something when we made love, Carrie?"

"Of course," she had smiled, one of her rare smiles, the polite one.

"Do you love me?" he had asked, feeling slightly foolish and surprised to hear himself ask her that.

"Yes."

Then he had said, "Was it the first time for you, Carrie? I couldn't tell."

"No."

"I'd never thought of that before, that you'd been to bed with a man before I met you."

"I think most girls have these days."

"Did you love him?"

"He was a blind date in college. I was quite drunk. I don't think I even knew his last name."

"Anyone else?"

"Slater, you're like a schoolboy . . . But no, no one else."

"You're a strange girl, Carrie."

"Why do you say that?"

"You seem to just take everything in your stride."

She had answered, "I try to."

So it went, so it went . . . and ultimately Slater took things in his stride as well, accepted her ways and their life, at times even thanked God it was devoid of petty quarrels and disorder. He was free to do most anything he wanted to, and he indulged himself in his freedom, and felt none of the contrition other men in his circumstances suffered, and if there were something missing between Carrie and himself, there was something there too which was missing in other couples: a certain calm, call it, a pattern which gave harmony and the peace of resignation to things as they are, and things seemed all right.

Until Jen.

Meeting Jen was like discovering a sixth sense in himself —a whole new faculty for feeling life. Before Jen, he had never even come close. He had never had a glimpse of the myriad shades of gaiety and solemnity which love could arouse, and he could look at her and touch her, and tell her about it, and she did that with him too. Both of them did, right from the start. His marriage then seemed like a long, complaisant prison sentence, with Jen as an unexpected reprieve. Every motion he went through with Carrie, he contrasted to his time with Jen, and he knew for certain that his marriage was unbearable any longer.

Carrie's death did not leave him remorseful. He was at first shocked at his own ease in the situation, and there were high euphoric sensations of having controlled his own destiny, without a pang of guilt, and it was easy too, to feel mere disinterest in Donald Cloward, almost as though by disposing of him, he had disposed of his own falsehoods to himself, and broken away from them. He became philosophic and insensitive to inner predictable impulses to be guilt-tinged and morbid, and he took life with Jen as though it were a prize for his sovereignty over such impulses.

He was rarely unhappy. When he was, he could not explain it to himself. It would come over him all of a sudden . . . maybe while he was out drinking beer at a lake place with Jen on a weekend, seeing himself in the mirror behind the bar, watching momentarily with fascination while his arm raised and lowered, the beer tipped into his mouth and there . . . was that good? He would feel depression start, prelude to a glimmering of crazy chaos: the plant going to pot; he would soon be 40; every weekend morning, a hangover; on and on—chaos without meaning, and Carrie's face then in the feeble rays of illusion, always smiling when she never had alive, smiling and smoking, and waiting for him to get his. . . . Maybe that way it came over him, and sometimes in other ways.

Once he had taken his secretary, Miss Rae, for a ride before he dropped her off at her home. It was autumn, and it was just an impulse. He long ago told himself he never had a kindly impulse; it was simply bare impulse, no explanation, but then they were driving to Hunter's Woods, and she was saying "O look at those leaves, and colors!" . . . He got out with her; he always kept a pistol in the glove compartment of his car. He liked to shoot from time to time, at cardboard targets he put to trees; sometimes at rats by the pier at the lake. An exercise, or a sport, from time to time. He shot at a tree, a tin can, a fence, and Miss Rae giggled and tittered beside him, and when he looked at her once, he saw her face flushed with happiness, and then she told him something her brother had said last week when he was visiting her. A bird had fallen into the pond in her back yard. O, she loved birds, don't misunderstand, and she was not laughing at the bird, but at what her brother said then. And she had been forced to stop in the midst of her story, while tears of mad laughter rolled down her cheeks. "My brother said, my broth—" and he had waited while more laughter frustrated her, thrilled her, then finally, "My brother said: 'Bird overboard!' " Then she had shaken with more fits of laughter, and the depression had begun rolling his way again, he could feel it coming at him. He drove her home. She got out of the car and said, "This has honestly been the most delightful afternoon I've ever spent, Mr. Burr!"

And on the way home, he had felt like taking the pistol from his glove compartment and shooting it through his brain.

He could not explain it. It was just there, and not very often, but intense when it was, like an incubus riding him in his sleep.

That morning he was close to it, but it was explainable that morning. Cloward's return had marred his sovereignty, intruded on it, and Carrie had come to his dreams to taunt him, worse for the fact he could not remember the dream. He watched Jen sleeping beside him, remembering last night's quarrel. He felt alone, and just as afraid as he always felt on the fringes of the depression. Someday it would come and not go. Then he would lose to it, and the inner doubts would grow and be big enough to throw off his control.

He wanted Jen then; desire spilled through him, as though he were clutching at all he could count on that had flesh and blood and heart. Quietly he moved over and pulled the covers back gently, touching the silk of her gown near her thighs, lifting the gown, putting his lips there. When she stirred, she touched his hair, murmured "darling," and finally, raised him up by the shoulders to her mouth, so that their mouths were pressed together in the last long finale.

He had gotten away; he felt himself come back, steady, steady.

"What a beautiful way to wake up, Slater."

His voice was even, the same. Good! "Yes," he said, "are you cold?"

"Hardly."

"Do you want a cigarette?"

"I think I'd like some more sleep."

"Okay," he said, "I think I'll have one . . . in the den."

"You can have one here, darling. I don't care."

"No, I'm too awake." He got up and straightened his pajamas, reached for his robe and slippers.

As he started out of the room, she said, "Slater?"

"What?"

"Thank you."

"Thank *you*," he said.

II.

Chayka took a cup of coffee back to the cell in the overnight lock-up. He turned the key in the door and walked across to the cot.

"Buzzy?"

Cloward rolled over and stared up at him. "Where am I?"

"Don't get excited. You're in jail."

"Oh, Gee-zus! Gee-zus!" Cloward sat bolt upright, rubbing his eyes, fixing his clothes.

Chayka set the coffee down on the stool beside the cot. "There aren't any charges," said Chayka. "It's all right, believe me."

"I vaguely remember . . . I was walking along Pine Avenue, wasn't I? *You're* a policeman, Ted?"

"Umm hmm. Surprise of the century, hmm? Yeah. I picked you up with Ernie Leogrande. Remember Ernie?"

"Sort of. Not well . . . I was at the Leydeckers, was that it?"

"The old man phoned in a complaint. He didn't want to press charges, or anything like that."

"What'd I do, anyway? I talked with Laura for a couple of seconds. I wasn't even in the house!"

"Well, he doesn't want you on his property. He says she doesn't want you there either."

"A lot he knows."

"Look," Chayka sat down beside him on the cot, "you're not planning to stay in Cayuta. Last night you said you you were cutting out, going to work in New York. If that's right, I'd just stay away from the Leydeckers, if I were you. Stay away from them, and don't talk about them, Buzzy. Open old wounds, is all . . . People have forgotten all about that."

"I know," Cloward sighed.

"I fixed things for you at home, too. I didn't think you'd want your old man in on this . . . so I called up Selma. I told her you were going to ride around with me."

"What did she say?"

"She said when were you going to get any sleep . . . I said you weren't sleepy. Being home was exciting, and you were wide awake."

"Thanks, Ted."

"I always liked you, Buzzy. You were trying to straighten up and fly right, way back when I was still drinking beer out at the pier and working down to Pat's Garage . . . I remember you socked me once, when I got fresh with Laura. 'Member that?"

"Yes. Thanks, Ted. I can't use any trouble."

"I began seeing the light a little while after you got sent up. I straightened myself out, with the help of Chris McKenzie, and—here I am."

"I saw McKenzie yesterday. At Walsh's Place."

"I know. That's another thing, Buzz . . . talking about what happened that night. I mean, at a place like Jitz's . . . It stirs things up, you know?"

"I know . . . How'd you hear about it?"

"My cousin. Al Secora. You know what Al's like. He's a flap-jaw, a sorehead."

"Well, I wasn't pouring out my troubles to him. I was talking with Mr. Burr, and he was butting in."

"Yeah, that's like him . . . but it's still no good to talk about all of it."

"I know. I got high."

"You on parole?"

"Yes."

"You're not even supposed to drink, are you?"

"No."

"You see, Buzzy, you just ask for trouble."

"You're right . . . I just had something to say to Mr. Burr. Something that's been bothering me for a long time. I just wanted to tell him about it."

"I heard a little about it. My advice is to forget it."

"Then . . . I was pretty drunk, I guess . . . I wanted to know about Laura. Ted, do you know anything about her? My sister says she's a recluse."

"Nobody ever sees Laura."

"Why? What's wrong with her?"

Chayka shook his head. "Your guess is as good as mine. I think she's a little balmy, you know? She always was a little balmy, Buzz."

"I can't understand it, though. She was going to college, I thought."

"For awhile, after you were sent up, she used to be around. I used to see her. Saw her once at the movies . . . But a few months later, you didn't see her around at all. I heard she was going to go to college, and for awhile we all thought she had . . . Then the rumors started she was up at the house on Highland Hill all the time. Just not coming out. I don't know."

"Ted," Cloward said, putting the coffee mug back on the stool, "I don't want to bother Mr. Leydecker. I have my own thoughts about him, but I don't want to get involved with him . . . I'd just like to see Laura once."

"Don't do it, Buzzy. He can make plenty of trouble for you. Plenty! You're on parole! If you go near there again, he'll get his back up. He made it clear he doesn't want you on his property."

Cloward sighed. "She wanted me to meet her tonight. Nine-thirty."

"I'm telling you, Buzzy, you could ruin everything for yourself."

"I don't know what to do . . . I just don't know."

"Call her up and tell her you can't make it, if you want, but don't go there."

"I know you're right. Mr. Burr wouldn't have anything to do with me any more, if he knew this." Buzzy took a sip of the coffee. "He's going to help me. I think I'm going to work for him."

"Yeah, you were talking about it last night in the car."

"Maybe I'm not worth his help. I don't know. Maybe I ought to stay out of Cayuta for good."

"Let me call Laura, Buzz. I'll tell her you can't come. Be better if I do it, in case Leydecker answers. If he answers, I'll just say you gave your word to me you wouldn't go near there again, and he could tell her . . . Simple. Doesn't implicate her or you—and if you are coming back to live here, I wouldn't have Leydecker for an enemy."

"Any more than he is now, you mean . . . I guess that's best."

"You haven't got it in for Leydecker, have you?"

"No. No, I guess not. I know I don't. I just want to forget it."

"That's best. It really is."

"Okay."

"Stay out of bars around here too, and keep your mouth shut, Buzz. Play it safe, until Mr. Burr gets it all fixed."

"Yes. Can I just walk out of here?"

"Now? Sure! I'm off duty, and I can run you home."

"You don't have to do that."

Chayka said, "It's not any trouble. I'm going up to see Chris McKenzie, and I go right past The Burr Building."

III.

The broadbacked figure drest in blue and green
Enchanted the maytime with an antique flute.
Blown hair is sweet, brown hair over the mouth blown
Lilac and brown hair;
Distraction, music of the flute, stops and steps of the
 mind over the third stair,
Fading, fading . . .

"What does it mean?"

"I don't know, Laura."

"Why did we come here?"

"To put my shirt by the lavender joe-pye weed."

"Why did you read that to me? What does it mean?"

He smiled and pulled her down, touched her blouse smiling, looked into her eyes: "Blown hair is sweet . . . over the mouth blown."

"Do you love me, Buzzy?"

He began to smile more, to laugh.

"Why are you laughing?"

He was laughing very hard, laughing with his hands cupping his mouth, mean laughing, the joke on her. He managed to say again, "Blown hair is sweet . . . over the mouth," but he was convulsed and could not finish.

"You *know!*"

"Yes. Yes, of course!"

She got up and ran, tripping over the shelf fungus with the D.C., L.L. carved on its face, and down through Hunter's Woods, naked and crying, with the crowds in between the trees, pointing, laughing the way he did.

She awakened to find Mrs. Basso's huge arms around her shoulders, her face crushed against Mrs. Basso's immense bosom.

"There, there, there."

She pulled away, and saw the book of Eliot poems on top of the pillow on her bed, where she had fallen asleep early this morning reading "Ash Wednesday." "Fading, fading, strength beyond hope and despair, climbing the third stair . . ."

"It's all right now," Mrs. Basso said. "Oh, Laura, honey, it's all, all right."

"All right, is it?" and she began to scream.

seventeen

Chris McKenzie slammed down the phone angrily. "That's all the thanks I get!" he said.

Lena was getting another glass of water at the sink, swallowing down more aspirin. She said, "Chris, the trouble is you boil everything down to drinking. You could have told Jen the gossip without the sermon about drinking thrown in. Everything doesn't boil down to drink!"

"Everything that has you running back and forth for water and aspirin this morning boils down to it, Lena."

"So I got a hangover . . . Hang out the flag! . . . Tell me what Chayka said about him and Nancy."

She sat down at the kitchen table and poured more coffee. She had heard everything Chayka had said about Secora's accusations against Slater, but that was a lot of blue mud. What she wanted to know was more about the problems Ted Chayka had with Nancy. Chris had given her the eye when Chayka started in on *that*. She had gone on into the living room, as she knew he wanted her to, and turned on the television. Still, she had been able to catch some of it, enough to be very titillated.

Chris said, "If I were to tell you that there was some truth to part of what Chayka was saying, what would you say then?"

"What part?"

"The part about Jen being mixed up with Slater *before* Carrie's death."

"How mixed with him? Sleeping together?"

"Uh huh. Sleeping together."

"And you knew it."

"Yes. All those times she was pretending to be out with Horace Dryden and the others, it was Slater. The whole summer, it was him."

"Holy Cow! Did Carrie know it?"

"I don't think so. If she did, she knew it the way she knew everything about Slater . . . she just passed over it. I don't know if she knew it or not."

"Well, how'd Al Secora know it?"

"I don't know that either. I don't know very much about this whole thing, but it's nasty gossip to be going around . . . Of course, Slater'll ignore it. Just go on drinking—the hell with it. But it'll hurt him, and it'll hurt Jen too."

Lena said, "I don't see that at all. You just found yourself another excuse to hit Slater about his drinking, s'all."

"One day he'll show up at one of our meetings. It's awfully hard to admit you're an alcoholic!"

"Yeah," Lena said, "but you make up for it later. Later it's all you can talk about."

"I talk about other things . . . Blue Eye, Chiggers, Rabies . . ."

"Distemper, Housebreaking, Worms," Lena finished the list. They both laughed.

Chris said, "Seriously though, it's nasty gossip."

"No one will give it a second thought, if you ask me. Oh, sure, they'll believe Slater and Jen were having an affair—that wouldn't surprise anyone who knew Slater, but this other stuff—it's silly."

"I agree, but I thought Jen should know what's being said."

"Tell me what Chayka said about Nancy."

"It wasn't all that important. They have problems."

"I can't imagine wanting to sleep with Nancy Chayka."

"You're probably not her type either, Lena."

"Is there another woman?"

"I think it's just the Seven Year Itch. He's lost interest. You know, Ted's a bright guy, and she's not exactly the high I.Q. type."

"Rubbish, Chris! Ted was Industrial High. Ten years ago he didn't know Q was in the alphabet."

"Well, he knows it now. That's my point. He's matured."

"Just because he joined AA?"

"Don't ride it too hard, Lena."

"All right, but the fact is, Nancy Chayka is a slob. She's let herself go."

The phone rang at that point and Lena said, "Doctor, my little dog is shivering and singing 'My Old Kentucky Home'. Does it mean anything?"

Chris said, "See if they pick it up at the hospital."

The phone stopped ringing, and Chris said, "They've got it . . . Slater never would have married Jen if Carrie hadn't been killed."

"It's her hair," said Lena. "I don't think Nancy Chayka's been to a beauty parlor in ten . . ."

Then the buzzer from the Animal Hospital signified the phone call was a personal one.

Chris got up and lifted the phone's arm from its wall bracket.

Slater Burr's voice said, "I've had it with you, Chris!"

"Slater?"

"Yes, Slater! I mean, this newest piece of slander is god-damned laughable!"

The look on Chris' face clued Lena to run into the bed-room and pick up the extension.

Chris said, "It isn't something I made up. I just thought Jen should know."

"I'm not only an alcoholic, I'm a murderer!"

"I just told Jen what Secora was yelling around Boyson's place last night, that's all. I thought Jen should know what yesterday's drinking expedition led to."

"I'm a murderer! Oh, that's a hot one, Chris!"

"I didn't say it. Needless to say, I discount it, but . . ."

"Oh, you'd love to believe that! You'd love to! Jesus Christ, what is wrong with you, Chris? You get Jen all excited just because we had a little fun at Walsh's Place yesterday, and your wife fell on her face!"

"Leave me out of it!" Lena's voice chimed in from the ex-tension.

"Then stay the hell out of it!"

"Yes, Lena," said Chris, "stay out of it!"

"He brought me into it! So I did fall on my face—you weren't so great yourself, Slater Burr!"

"Le-na!" Chris shouted. "Hang up the phone!"

"The next time you get any bright ideas about me," Slater said, "just tell them to me and leave Jen out of it!"

"She happens to be my sister, Slater."

"We'll be more than happy to leave you both alone," Lena McKenzie said.

There was a click.

Chris said, "Slater?"

"He hung up," said Lena.

"Look, Miss Busy-Body, did you have to butt in?"

"My dog has fleas!" Lena sang out, "Doctor McKenzie? My dog has . . ."

"Oh, for God's sake, Lena!" He dropped the phone and went back and sat at the kitchen table.

When Lena waltzed in, he said, "You should have stayed out of it!"

"Boy, was his dander up!"

"I know," said Chris. "It's funny, because Jen just laughed off the whole thing."

"She probably had a delayed reaction."

"I know Jen better than that. She wasn't at all excited. I never thought Slater would think twice about it. I thought Jen might, but not him . . . Well, that's the thanks I get."

Lena sat down and picked up her cup of coffee. After a moment she said, "When was the last time they slept together?"

"Now how the hell would I know that, Lena! My sister doesn't . . ."

"No. I mean Nancy and Ted," Lena McKenzie said.

II.

Selma was already at work when Donald Cloward got back to the apartment. His father took a coffee break and sat with Cloward at the table in the living room.

"The thing about Olinski," Milton Cloward was saying, "is that he wants to please me. Now, a lot of fellows run the thing without thinking. Just another job to a lot of fellows. But Olinski remembers little pointers I give him, like Keller Insurance on seven, likes to have the operator ask a passenger getting off 'You going to Keller?' Then point out the office to anyone going there, you know, son?"

"Yes, pop, I know."

"You see, Keller is just around the corner to the left, and people miss it. Sometimes just go right back down. Could lose business that way . . . But Olinski always remembers to ask, 'You going to Keller?' . . . I put him on Car 2, you know, right before the holidays."

"You told me, pop."

"He looks up to me. It's only natural to feel something for The Starter, but Olinski don't just think of me as boss. He's got a real notion to please me, you know, son?"

"Sure, pop."

"That's why I went to his place Christmas Eve. You shoulda seen his face when I come in the door, son, he . . ."

Cloward sat there half-listening, with a loneliness all through him now. He was very tired, physically tired, and tired too of his father's perpetual talk about the job and

Olinski. He realized the same thing he knew when he sat listening to Guy: he was not in the picture at all. His only hope was Slater Burr, and last night he had almost destroyed that with his drunken visit to Laura Leydecker. He had to prove to Slater that he was a different person from the dumb kid eight years back, quick and ambitious and through with his past; that was his one chance, convincing Slater Burr of that.

He had no interest in being Guy Gilbert's secretary; the very idea of being a secretary repelled him. Nor did he have any enthusiasm about working in a huge city where he would count for nothing, with his prison record and his lack of education. But working for Mr. Burr he could climb fast, exactly as Mr. Burr had done, working for Nelson Stewart.

In prison for a year he had had a cell mate who was keen on psychology. He used to discuss with him the fact Slater Burr sent a Christmas card every year.

His cell mate had said, "Maybe this Burr wished his wife dead."

"What sense would that make?"

"A lot. You did what he might have done himself, so in a way he's grateful to you, because you saved him from doing it. It's not unusual."

"He was crazy about her."

"You never know, Don . . . Then too, lots of breaks a guy gets here, he gets from the people he did the most damage to on the outside. I've seen it happen. I knew a murderer once, his only visits at the end were from the victim's sister. It makes some people feel big as hell to forgive. They feel like little gods!"

Cloward did not accept the theory because he was not sure he understood it, but he never lost the idea that when he got out he would at least straighten out one fact: he was sure he had not stolen Slater Burr's car that night. It was like an obsession with him. He went over and over the conversation he would have with Mr. Burr, and he did not pretend to himself that it was all he wanted. He never lost the hope that Slater Burr might say, "We have a place for you in the plant, Buzzy, if you want it."

Once or twice, he even imagined Leydecker making the same offer; Leydecker saying, "All right, you and I know I gave you the keys, and you and I know that at the last minute I moved you to Slater Burr's car, hoping you'd hit the drop-off. I'm ready to make it up to you."

But that was a fantasy, no thread of likelihood there. Leydecker had no sympathy for Cloward's kind; Slater Burr, on the other hand, was cut from the same cloth. If Nelson Stewart had been a snob, Slater Burr could easily have been in Donald Cloward's shoes. There was the difference, to Cloward's mind.

Now it was beginning to work out, wasn't it? If he could just keep hold of himself, watch impulses, and drinking that inspired them . . . keep hold, and play everything exactly as Slater Burr had told him to . . . But in the back of his thoughts that morning was the fear Slater Burr would get wind of what he had done last night, after Mrs. Burr dropped him off, or that he would simply change his mind . . . that something like that would go wrong.

His father said, "Well, son, I best be getting back."

He looked at the old man. He wanted to be a lot more than Milton Cloward, a lot more than a male secretary too.

"I think I'll sleep," he said.

"Did you have an exciting night with Ted?"

"Sort of."

"We was worried when you didn't come home for so long. Of course, we knew better than to think you'd get in any trouble, but . . ."

"I saw some old friends, was all."

He felt the urge to tell his father he had been with the Burrs. He wondered if his father would react with anything but worry that his son would get into trouble again; it all came down to that . . . No, he would wait.

"I never thought Ted Chayka'd make anything of himself, but it goes to show you . . . How long you staying on, son?"

He felt like saying don't worry, pop, I'll get out of your way as fast as I can.

"A day or two. I'm not sure yet."

"We're glad to have you."

"Thanks, pop."

"After all, this is your home."

"Yes."

"I best be getting back, or Olinski will be The Starter before I know it! Got to keep my eye on Olinski," his father chuckled.

III.

Anyone else might have taken the rest of the day off, or

waited until the union took action, but Mona Sontag could only think in terms of finding a new job immediately. She had already missed her first Christmas Club payment, and with Burr sick, and the terramycin Dr. McKenzie had advised, so expensive, her dismissal that noon had rocked her into a panic. Behind the panic was: *I told you so, Mona.*

In a way she did not even wonder why she was fired. She was the sort of person who gave money to the Cancer Fund out of fear that refusal to contribute would lead to cancer . . . Over and over yesterday, she had told herself two things: don't get mixed up with people you're not in a class with, and don't give in to Albert Secora just because he bought you such an expensive present . . . She had not listened to herself on either count. She had gone right on drinking with the Burrs and the McKenzies up at Jitz's, and when Al took her home, she had let him do it on the couch in her parlor. She had brushed her doubts and rules aside, and now she was paying for it.

The personnel director at Leydecker Electric studied her application form.

He said, "Ten years at Burr Manufacturing Company?"

"Ten years," said Mona Sontag.

"And you were fired just like that? For no reason?"

"The reason given," said Mona Sontag, "was that the office was overstaffed." God punished, was all. *But I will punish you according to the fruit of your doings, saith the Lord.*

"Right at Christmas time," Mr. Percy, the personnel man said, "and right in the middle of the day . . . That seems strange."

"I was given two weeks severance pay," Mona Sontag said, to emphasize that if she had done something very wrong, she would have been let go without pay, as Linda Hadley had been let go, for stealing from petty cash.

"Were you the only one let go?"

"The only one from the office," she hedged. It made no sense to feel shame at being fired along with Al, but she felt shame anyway, because of letting him do it last night . . . all so shoddy, there on the couch in her parlor, drunk. There was no point in trying to figure out Slater Burr's reasoning. She had been too drunk to remember what had taken place in the latter part of the afternoon, at Jitz's, and she no longer cared. God had punished, and now she needed a new job.

"Then others were fired, in the plant?"

"I heard some talk about it, but I can't say for sure."

"Miss Sontag," Mr. Percy said, "would you mind very much waiting here a moment?"

Mona Sontag gave him a defeated smile, a shrug. "I got all day."

Some holidays these were turning out to be! Burr with the Blue Eye, and herself cheapened and out of a job. *I told you so, Mona,* she thought, while she waited for Mr. Percy to return.

eighteen

Min's solemn eyes watched from the leather frame on his desk, as Kenneth Leydecker finished his telephone conversation with Mrs. Basso.

"The doctor gave her some tranquilizers," said Mrs. Basso, "and they've quieted her down, sir, but she wants to be sure you talked with the Cloward boy, as you promised."

"That's all taken care of," he said. Min's eyes seemed to sharpen with disappointment at the lie, and Leydecker looked away from her face, and down at the report on his desk. ". . . the probable sales volume will be more than $9,000,000 for the company this year compared with $4,250,000 last year." He said into the phone's mouthpiece: "This is a very busy time for me, but I'd come home if it'd help, Mrs. Basso."

"No, sir, I think it'd make everything worse. I think the girl wants to be alone, is what I think. His coming back like this has started it all up again, sir."

"I know . . . I know . . . Did Doctor Yates say anything else?"

"Just to keep her doped up until things pass over, sir."

"Is she eating, at least?"

"Nothing, sir."

"I see . . . Well, you've done all you can, Mrs. Basso, and I appreciate it."

"I'm sorry, sir. It's such a shame."

"Yes," Leydecker said, "call me if there's anything important."

He hung up, and looked back at Min's photograph. "It wouldn't have done any good to talk to the boy!" he said aloud to her. "The police know how to . . ." his voice trailed off, and he shook his small body from his thoughts, shuffled through his papers, and gave Leydecker Electric and The City of Cayuta his attention . . . At least the day had brought one good, positive thing Kenneth Leydecker's way. In the morning mail, a letter from The Ithaca Lock Corporation. They were highly interested in Leydecker's very confidential proposal for a merger with Burr Manufac-

turing Company. Their plant outside Ithaca was amply
equipped to accommodate a merger, and their tentative esti-
mate was much more than Slater Burr could hope for from
any other concern. If Leydecker could squeeze Burr out via
the zoning proposal, Burr would have no choice but to accept
I.L.C.'s offer. It was a coup for Leydecker, no doubt of that;
quite different from leaving Burr with no alternative, which
would make Leydecker look like the villain . . . He would
rid Cayuta of its foremost eyesore in center town, enhance
Cayuta to G.E., then work for Leydecker Electric's merger
with G.E. . . . Very neat and sound, but there would be
plenty of careful work on Leydecker's part.

Leydecker had already warned Oliver Percy not to hire
any more employees from Burr Manufacturing Company.
A representative from I.L.C. was arriving in Cayuta next
week, all on the sly, to look over Burr Company. Leydecker
wanted no labor disputes there . . . everything in order. No
one wanted to buy anyone else's bitter draft. Burr Company
was worth little enough, without the added distraction of
labor trouble. Even though that would not affect I.L.C. after
a merger, it looked bad.

After Burr and The Cayuta Macaroni Company were gone,
Cayuta would be a decent city. The day was past when a
small city could exist on its home-grown industry; all the
big money was on the outside. The thing was, to pull it in,
and that was what Kenneth Leydecker intended to do—pull
it in! The trouble with Slater Burr's kind was that they did
not want to work for anyone else; they were living back in
the forties, when there was a war and war contracts . . . The
trouble with small cities categorized as "depressed areas"
was they did not gang up on the Slater Burrs—force them
to act . . . Well, Kenneth Leydecker would do it for Cayuta,
and Kenneth Leydecker would come out just as nicely as
Cayuta would.

He picked up the inter-office phone at a buzz, and listened
to Oliver Percy.

"Send her up," he said. "I'll talk to her myself."

And that was part of it too . . . reaching everyone, big and little alike, having time for a secretary named Miss Sontag, the same as for Hamilton Carruth, from Ithaca Lock.

II.

"Oh, you're just drunk!" Francie Boyson said. "How'd you get so drunk in the middle of the day?"

She wished he would hang up. She was sitting in the banister-back arm chair with a glass of beer and an egg-and-olive at her elbow, trying to follow *Search For Tomorrow* on the television at the same time she talked to him. Thank God it was Rich's day to buy the week's meat for the restaurant, and he was downtown doing just that right now.

"Well, did we or did we not see them up at Blood Neck making out? Just answer me that, Francie."

"What're you doing drunk and talking all over about that? That's over and done with. I been true to Rich ever since then, and I don't like it being dragged in, after all this time!"

"Francie, if I told you that you might be a murder witness some day, in a murder trial, what'd you say to that?"

"I'd say you was having more of your drunken pipe dreams, is what I'd say!" But she put down her glass of Budweiser, leaned across, and turned down the sound on the set.

"This is no pipe dream, Francie! I'm collecting evidence!"

"Oh, yeah? I'm collecting stamps!"

"Slater Burr murdered Carrie Burr, to marry Jen McKenzie . . . Now! How does that set with you, Francie?"

"Get outa here!" Francie Boyson said. Then she turned the set off altogether. "Get outa here!" she repeated, eager . . . waiting for Al Secora to continue.

III.

At noon, Walter Olinski had a three-hour break before he was back on Car 2. Sometimes he went home, ate lunch and lounged around the house; other times, he took the bus up to the P.W.V. club, drank some beer and played the pinballs. Today he had done the latter, and instantly, as he walked in the door, he regretted it.

It was The Club's fault, for letting non-members come there, just because they were Polish, and The Club needed the money. Al Secora was no war veteran! Walter Olinski had fought in The First World War, and he resented the way outsiders like Secora came into the P.W.V. and threw their weight around, as though they'd broken the Hindenburg line single-handed!

What irked Olinski even more, as he strolled into the bar, was the fact Secora was sounding off about Milt Cloward's kid.

Milt Cloward was a Prince, one of the greatest guys Olinski had ever come across, and while Olinski did not hear everything Secora was saying, he did hear Secora say, "And Buzzy Cloward will get it next! Me and Mona got fired, and there's no telling what Slater Burr will do to Buzzy Cloward!"

"Yeah, yeah," Brushkin, the bartender was humoring him, "but I'd sober up before I made any more phone calls, Al."

"Gimme some more dimes," Secora said. "Next I'm calling Cloward. Don't think he's not going to get the axe from Slater Burr!"

Olinski said quietly, "That's all you know."

"What's that mean?" Secora said, turning to face him.

"Mr. Burr is very fond of that boy, for your information."

"Sure, pop, and you won the second battle of the Marne. We heard all about it."

"Donald Cloward is going to make something out of himself," said Olinski. "More than you'll do . . . not even a member here."

"He'll make something out of himself if Slater Burr don't get him first. C'mon, Brushy, gimme some more dimes. I'm collecting myself some evidence."

Olinski said, "Mr. Burr has asked Donald Cloward to stay at his place. I happen to know that for a fact."

"He's *what?*"

"Milt told me right before I went off. He was real proud because Mr. Burr's taking an interest in Donald. Him and Mrs. Burr asked the boy up to their place to stay. Your talk don't amount to nothing, never did. You don't belong here at the P.W.V."

Secora said, "You got shell-shock, old man. Don't know what you're talking about any more."

"Oh, I know what I'm talking about. Milt told me right before I went off. 'Whatta you think of that, Olinski,' he says, 'Slater Burr's taking a personal interest in Donald' . . .

Well, I says, I think that's swell! And that's what I do think. You just want to make trouble, Albert Secora."

"What's this about them moving Buzzy in?" Secora said.

"Surprise you that there are decent people, Albert?" Olinski said back. Then he turned away from Secora, and went back toward The Trophy Room, where he could have a beer and look through the magazines in peace.

IV.

"But Mr. Leydecker," said Oliver Percy. "I don't have any idea where he'd be. I don't relate to his sort at all."

"Did you call Boyson's?"

"Of course. It was the first place I called, sir. Then I called Walsh's Place, and O'Conners, and the pool hall."

"And his home?"

"No answer."

"He wouldn't still be hanging around Burr Company?"

"I tried there too, sir . . . It seems to me, sir, that we can hardly be accused of unfair employment practices if we hire people Mr. Burr has fired!"

"I don't care how it seems to you, Oliver! Don't hire anyone from Burr Company. Miss Sontag said just the two of them were let go for no reason. Now, I don't like the looks of it."

"He's fired people before, sir . . . She had very dirty fingernails."

"Oliver, Al Secora is big in the union at B.M.C., and she's worked there for ten years! Firing them both in the middle of the day doesn't make sense! It sounds to me like Slater Burr is building for a strike! Otherwise, there's no sense to it."

"Why would he want a strike?"

"Someone might have tipped him off about I.L.C. . . . I don't know why he wants one, but he's asking for one, that's clear!"

"Yes, sir . . . I'll keep trying to locate Secora, Mr. Leydecker, but I truly don't relate to his sort at all!"

"You'd better start relating to his sort! His sort is what we have to deal with! I can convince Secora, if I can get my hands on him. He's pliable, and he doesn't like Slater Burr."

"Could Secora stop a strike?"

"He could if he just said he didn't want the job anyway. The union won't fight for a man who doesn't want the job, and I'll see to it that Secora won't need the job. We won't hire him . . . his name won't be on our payroll, but we'll take care of him," Kenneth Leydecker said, "if you just *find* him, before he ruins everything!"

V.

Everything **had** gone so well that morning . . . right until Chris called.

It had **been** the first time, in a long time, that Slater had made love to her twice. He had awakened her that way; then he had come back an hour later. He had loved her very slowly and well. There was something poignant and special about it . . . sometimes there was, and the second time had been one of those times . . . Afterward, they had smoked cigarettes, the bedsheet covering them, the first circle of morning sun spotting their pillow.

"I must have dreamed of Carrie," Slater had said. "I felt low when I first woke up."

"It's Donald Cloward being back."

"I suppose . . . That was stupid yesterday, bringing him here —getting involved with him at Walsh's."

"Do you think there's anything to his story?"

"No. I was humoring him along."

"And the job you promised to get him?"

"More of the same. But in the den I was thinking," Slater said, "I think I'll give him some money, get him out of my hair and back to New York."

"Yes . . . Is he coming for dinner tonight?"

"The hell with it! I'll tell him to come to my office and give him the money. He can get the sleeper tonight."

"We'll have dinner alone."

"I'd like that," said Slater.

Chris had called while Slater was showering. What he told her made Jen laugh. God, what next, would people think of to say about Slater!

Jen had said, "Was I supposed to be off hiding in the bushes, like Carole Tregoff, Chris? Just think what a sensation it'll be in Cayuta! Another Finch trial!"

"Jen, it isn't funny! I know there's nothing to it, but it's nasty gossip. Prepare yourself."

"I'm ready to swear in court that Slater and I fell in love the second we laid eyes on one another! And if the Cloward boy hadn't done in Carrie, well, we might very well have! Okay?"

She had felt very pleased, lying there in bed, full of Slater, full of him and glad to announce possession of him, right from the start.

She had a smile on her face. She felt high and gay, superior to Chris's world of if-you-knew-what-people-were-saying, and drink-will-be-his-downfall. While she let Chris babble on in his old maid's tone of portentous anxiety, she planned to go down and make a Bloody Mary for Slater, have it ready for him when he came out of the shower. He was a magnificent man; his magnificence was stamped all over her; God, she bet not another woman anywhere felt as Jen Burr felt right then!

When Slater came from the shower with a towel around him, a grin cut across his face as she handed him the drink.

"Happy this morning," she said, "and get ready for a good laugh, darling."

And then . . . all hell had broken loose.

She had never seen Slater act that way before; it was as though something had snapped in him.

He had called Chris back, and the house had shaken with his shouting.

He had refused breakfast, hurried into his clothes, and gone off to work in the station wagon, hardly saying anything to her.

After she pulled herself together, she was able to realize that her suspicions were accurate, right to the letter. Slater *did* feel guilty about Carrie's death; it was not just a sore point, it was a malignancy.

Around eleven o'clock, he called to apologize. He sounded more like himself, but there was still a peppering of hysteria in what he said. He had talked to Cloward. Cloward was coming to dinner that evening, and Slater was putting him on the sleeper to New York at eleven P.M.

"Don't mention it to Chris," he said, "or to anyone."

"Very hush-hush, hmmm?"

"Goddam it, Jen, that silly tone in your voice is irritating! I'm trying to get something done about this thing!"

"You're not really concerned about the talk, are you, Slater?"

"I just want Cloward out of here!"

It was best all the way around. As Jen drove the Jaguar to pick up Donald Cloward, she realized that. It was what the boy wanted, and it was best for Slater too. There had been enough pressure on Slater these past few months;

Cloward's return was the catalyst to a minor crack-up in Slater . . . because what else could it be called?

Jen turned onto Genesee Street, and stopped before The Burr Building. She watched while Donald Cloward came out, carrying his bags, his father hovering in the background, waving at Jen, smiling.

Jen heard Cloward say, "See you later, pop."

While Cloward put his bags in the jump seat, Jen said, "You're not angry with one another, Don?"

"No, not at all."

"I just wondered . . . the way you said 'goodbye'."

"He thinks I'm going to spend a few days with you, before I leave for New York. He doesn't know I'm taking the sleeper tonight. I thought I'd write him a letter when I got to your place. If I try to tell him, he'll just feel bad that he didn't make me welcome, or something. Both him and Selma . . . Mr. Burr said it was better this way, to write a letter."

Jen said, "Do you want to drive, Donald?"

"Gee, sure!"

He came around to the left side of the car and got in.

"It's great of you and Mr. Burr to do this for me," he said . . . Then, for a few moments, he sat working with the shift, to figure it out, before he could make the Jaguar go.

nineteen

The luminous dial on the alarm clock by the bed read four-twenty. Ted Chayka rolled over on his side and thought about his dream. It had been the same old one. In it, he always failed the police examinations and had to go back to Pat's Garage and beg for his old job.

"Don't try to be what you're not," Pat always said, at the end, and Chayka always woke up, just as Pat's grease-stained hand reached out to touch him.

There was a faint odor of stale beer in the room. Chayka did not have to guess where it came from. Nancy had left one of her ubiquitous empty cans beside the bed last night. This morning, when Ted came into the bedroom to go to sleep, he had found the bed unmade, as usual, and covered with last night's newspapers, the *TV Guide,* and more nail-polish peelings.

He thought of his talk with Chris that morning. He had complained to Chris about the way Nancy did that—peeled off her polish that way, and Chris had said it was a nervous sign. Probably Nancy was as nervous as Ted was, Chris had said. What they both needed was a long candid talk together.

While Nancy and he ate breakfast, before he had come in to sleep, he had tried.

"Nance," he had said, "what do you think about us?"

"What do you mean?"

"I mean, do you think we're as good together as we used to be?"

"In bed, or what?"

"In every way," Chayka said. "In *every* way, Nancy."

Nancy had answered: "You been itching for a fight all week, Ted, so you might as well get it off your chest! What's the matter? You still burned because I didn't send your uniform to the cleaners last Tuesday?"

He had dropped it there. A long candid talk with Nancy was as likely as hot snow or cold fire; he might as well have a long candid talk with the kitchen sink . . . Then, it occurred to Ted Chayka that there was someone else he was supposed to have a talk with . . . someone else, and finally, he remembered. He was to call the Leydeckers, tell whoever answered, that Buzzy Cloward was not coming by there again.

Chayka reached for the phone, and started to dial, when he heard Nancy's voice on the wire.

". . . . wouldn't surprise me," she was saying, "nothing would about Slater Burr. But do you know for sure, Francie?"

"Well, I happen to know first hand they was having an affair, summer of 1954, but I can't say *how* I know. I just know for sure."

"I'm not surprised," said Nancy. "But how'd the Cloward boy get in the car?"

"I heard he was put in the car. Slater Burr put him in it!"

Oh, for the love of Christ! Chayka banged the phone down and got out of bed. He put his trousers on over his shorts and reached for his shirt on the back of the chair. Then he slid into his socks and shoes and went into the living room.

"Hang up that phone!" he said.

Nancy said, "Count Dracula is awake! I gotta hang up, Francie."

When she put down the phone, Chayka said, "That's nice gossip! Dammit, Nancy, I want you to cut it out!"

"For your information, Ted, Francie Boyson called *me*. I didn't call her!"

"What the hell is wrong with you anyway, Nancy? Don't you know the Burrs can sue for that kind of talk?"

"Are they tapping everyone's wires now? That wouldn't surprise me! Where you going?"

"Out." Chayka grabbed his coat and scarf from the hook in the hall.

"It's all over town anyways. They going to sue the whole city of Cayuta?"

"You believe that gossip, and next you'll believe the earth is flat!"

"Where are you taking yourself off to, middle of the afternoon?"

"I have an errand," he said.

There was no sense chancing Nancy's overhearing a call to the Leydeckers. God alone knew what she would make of that!

II.

Mona Sontag was mad at Father Gianonni. She had said

her Act of Contrition and the Hail Marys, but she left St. Anthony's angrily. Father Gianonni had yawned during her confession. That was a man for you—just yawn it off, same way Al Secora just pushed her back on the couch right there in the parlor. Never mind making it nice, taking it seriously. One damn man was just like another. God was already punishing her, and if a priest was not going to take the sin seriously, he was not going to have it in his power to forgive her. The mumbo-jumbo would not get her off the hook, not if the priest had no interest. Half of it was up to the priest. At the end of the confession, when he had said, "Pray for me, my child," she had felt like saying back, "Oh yeah? Why should I do *you* any favors?" . . . But she had said a prayer for him, a very quick one, since she was not a type to take chances with Fate.

Mr. Leydecker had been very nice about all of it, but he was not about to hire her. Big as life out front of Leydecker Electric was a sign saying "Office Help Needed," but he was not about to hire Mona Sontag. All that talk about not hiring help from another industry in Cayuta was just claptrap . . . and since when . . . since when! Leydecker Electric had even hired Linda Hadley, a known thief! . . . But not Mona Sontag!

All Mona could think of was that Al must have really fixed them, the last hour at Jitz's place. She had a lot of trouble remembering anything about that time; she had not really come to until Al was fumbling with her clothes in the parlor. Oh, God, and the things he had done too—things no man had ever done to Mona Sontag, and there weren't *that* many men in the first place. She had never been punished this much before, and she could not blame God!

"I didn't know, God," she said to herself as she walked down Capitol Street. "How was I to know he was some kind of pervert!"

Ah, but that was no excuse. No excuse. She let him, was all, and now she was like a piece of dirt.

At Acme Drugs, she stopped to buy terramycin for poor Burr. She was nearly in tears now, thinking of Burr with the Blue Eye, and herself in the state she was in: ". . . *and I detest my sins above every evil, because they displease Thee.*" . . . The thing was, how *long* were they going to displease Him?

She waited for the druggist to get her the medicine, and then she found herself staring at the phone booth, back by the soda fountain. She looked up at the big clock—four-thirty, and she thought to herself: *He* wouldn't be home yet. I could just say, Mrs. Burr, ma'am, I'm sorry about yesterday . . .

That was all . . . I'm sorry about yesterday. If God and the priests weren't going to help her, she would have to help herself. While she fumbled in her change purse for a dime, she took it back about God not helping her; it wasn't fair, and it wasn't very safe to think along those lines. No, God was okay . . . and there was a dime. The trouble with Father Gianonni was he drank all the communion wine, and was half-asleep most of the time, as a result.

Bravely, she walked back and shut herself inside.

"Hello?"

"Hello, Mrs. Burr?"

"Yes."

"This is Mona Sontag, from Walsh's Place. I mean, from yesterday at Walsh's Place. Remember?"

"Oh yes, Mona, how are you?"

"I'm fine . . . I'm not fine, exactly. I'm sorry, Mrs. Burr, ma'am, about yesterday."

"Mona, we were all celebrating Christmas. You have nothing to be sorry about."

"Well, I don't remember it very well."

"Mona, we were all in the same condition. There's no reason to feel badly."

The tears gathered in Mona's eyes then. She said, "I been ten years with B.M.C., ma'am. My dog is even named Burr. I just—don't know what to say, but if I did something yesterday to cause . . ." and her voice broke, and she fished in her coat pocket for a tissue.

"Cause what, Mona?"

"Cause Mr. Burr to fire me, ma'am."

"Mr. Burr *fired* you?"

"He said the office was overstaffed, but Mrs. Burr, there's work enough there for ten girls."

"I don't understand. Are you sure that was the reason?"

"No, ma'am, because he fired Al Secora too, so I thought . . ."

"I see."

"I thought it was something I did yesterday, or Al."

"Mona," Mrs. Burr said gently, "let me talk to Mr. Burr when he comes in."

"I tried to get another job, but . . ."

"You're upset now, Mona. You just forget about it until I talk with Mr. Burr. Then I'll call you, tonight, at your home. All right?"

"All right, Mrs. Burr."

There was a click, and Mona Sontag said a feeble, futile "goodbye" to the dial tone, hung up, and let herself out the booth.

III.

Only last night, Oliver Percy had said he should have a raise, for all Kenneth Leydecker was expecting of him lately. He had not said it to Kenneth Leydecker; he would prefer to forget the person to whom he had said it, but even if there had been a bit of braggartry in his long harangue over a glass of sherry late, latè last night, this afternoon was proof enough his complaint was justified . . . Here it was five-thirty already, but forget all about *that*; look who he was here in center town traffic with!

Finally, he had located him at the Polish War Veterans Club. He was to deliver him to Leydecker Electric, where Leydecker was waiting to talk with him . . . Well, that would be a pretty talk, you can bank on that! In *his* condition! . . . They were driving through downtown traffic, and it was no easy task to steer, with Secora clapping his arms on Oliver Percy's shoulders and breathing his foul breath in Percy's furious face!

"Tell you what, buddy," Secora was saying, "we're gonna have a strike *and* a trial, hah? . . . Oh, ask not what Slater Burr can do to you, but what you can do to Slater Burr! Hah? J.F.K. . . . Hah? . . . Hey—knock, knock!" Secora rapped Oliver Percy's shoulder with his knuckle. "Knock, knock!" he repeated.

"Please!" said Percy, "this is five o'clock traffic."

I'm hardly a Personnel Director, Percy had said, only last night, *my title should be Executive Confidant!*

"You know what I did last night, Mr. Percy-O? First time I ever did it to a woman, see. You gotta be a little boozed up, see. I—"

"I *don't* care to hear about it, thank you!"

"Well, ain't that the old nose-in-air fer you!"

"I'm trying to drive this car safely."

"Someone ought to pin a rose on you for that, Percy. Hey, knock, knock!"

"Will you stop punching me, please?"

Percy swung the car over to the curb, near L.E.'s downtown hiring center. Somehow, he was supposed to propel this person up to Kenneth Leydecker's office!

"Who's there? Astronaut," Secora was talking to himself, "astronaut if Slater Burr killed his wife, but ask what your country can do for you!"

"Oh, shush! Shush!" Oliver Percy shrieked, and by now, the five o'clock crowds were thick in front of the place . . . gradually, a few here, a few there, turning to stare.

It was an immense embarrassment for Oliver Percy even to be seen in the company of Secora; after all, he could *hardly* turn to the onlookers and say, "This is all part of my duties, you understand!"

Percy felt sudden relief when he saw Ted Chayka walking toward the car.

IV.

". . . So we come, to the end, of a per-fect day," Miss Rae sang to herself as she covered the typewriter and dropped her pencils in the white mug on her desk, just outside Mr. Burr's office . . . A bit of irony at day's end, she mused . . . per-fect day, indeed! Perfectly preposterous! . . . Ah, and the dear lamb in there so sorry about all of it now . . . How many times had he buzzed her to see if she had gotten hold of Mona Sontag yet!

"Don't worry, sir," she told him each time, dear heart, don't worry, "I'll locate her. She's probably in some café."

"Keep trying Secora too, Miss Rae. Tell them both it was a mistake."

Yes, lambie, and we all make them. "Yes, sir," she had answered.

Well, she would certainly have enough to fill a page or two in her diary this evening.

She planned the beginning: "I knew instantly that something was wrong when he walked in this morning. His dear blue eyes were sunk deep in . . ."

The door of the reception room swung open, and a young man in a leather jacket stood there, a cigarette dangling from his lips. Well, if it isn't Marlon Brando, Miss Rae said to herself. She liked her little mind jokes. The obituary of her daydreams read: "Behind the spinsterish façade of Millicent

Marvin Rae, was a rollicking good humor, and a quick and full heart."

She said to the young man, "The office is closed."

"I want to see Slater Burr."

"If wishes were horses," Miss Rae answered, "beggars might ride."

"Is he still here, or isn't he?"

"He is. But you have no appointment, and if it's employment you're seeking, the employment office is on the first floor, to the right of the door as you enter, and *it* will be open at 8:30 in the morning."

"I'll wait for him to come out." The young man sat down in one of the leather chairs.

Miss Rae said, "This office is closed, young man."

"Has he got someone in there with him?"

"That is none of your business."

"Uh huh. Well, I'll wait, Miss, if you don't mind. I'll just sit here quietly and wait for him to come out."

"It won't get you anywhere . . . What do you want with Mr. Burr anyway?"

"That is none of your business, Miss. I'll wait."

"Wait. You won't bother me," said Miss Rae.

But it did bother her, which was one reason she did not pick up the inter-office and tell Mr. Burr he was there. Heaven knows what the young man wanted, but Miss Rae knew Mr. Burr would probably tell her to just go along, he'd take care of it. Then she would miss her ride home with him . . . *Dear, dear* heart, our time together is so fleeting—moments stolen from the years in inches . . . Ah lamb, and tonight he needed her, so upset and all, his cherished brow furrowed in frowns and worries. There, there, it's not that bad.

"We all get out of sorts, sir," she had planned to say, as he drove her down Genesee Street. "And I've seldom seen you lose your temper so. You were due. We're all due a day like that, sir."

And he would say, "What about you, though, Miss Rae . . . in all the years I've known you, you've never once . . ."

"Ah, never mind an old maid, sir. But I have my days too, sir." Days near you, lamb.

The young man said, "When's he usually come out?"

"Oh, this time sometimes, sometimes later . . . sometimes six, and sometimes seven."

"Tell him I'm waiting then. Tell him that."

"I can't disturb him, young man. Those are my orders."

"Do *you* hang around until he leaves?"

Always . . . waiting, hoping: *Miss Rae, can I drop you? . . .* She said, "I do my work. When my work is done, I go home."

Tonight, after the evening ritual—the cooking dinner, sweeping, bathing, preparing clothes for the next day, then: the diary, writing in it at her desk, in her nightie and robe, with her hair pinned in rags: "Today, he must have had a fight with her. There's no other explanation. Two people were fired. I never saw him in such a rage."

Marlon Brando was stubbing out his cigarette impatiently. Just go on! Just leave! She said, "I think he'll be very late today, young man," but her words were punctuated by the opening of his door.

The young man stood up. "Mr. Burr? Mr. Slater Burr?"

"Yes."

"I'd like to talk with you, Mr. Burr."

"What about?"

That's a lamb; don't give him the time of day; O I'm waiting, see me, dear?

"It's personal, if you don't mind . . ." looking now in Miss Rae's direction. She went right on putting away her things, ostensibly oblivious, and he would say: "Anything you have to say can be said in front of Miss Rae."

Slater Burr said, "Miss Rae?"

"Yes, sir?"

"Why don't you just run along now. Why, it's after five-thirty!"

Sometimes, though, it was after six, remember? And I was always here, lamb, and today when you need reassurance, I wanted to . . .

"Yes, sir, I'm leaving now," said Millicent Rae.

twenty

"All right," said Slater Burr, "fifty dollars, but how the hell do *you* know Oliver Percy?"

"That's my business. I just want to get out of this town. You hand over the money, and I'll say my little spiel, and we'll call it even, okay?"

"Thirty, forty, fifty," Slater counted out the bills and slapped them to Miss Rae's desk. "All right, I'm waiting."

"Percy claims this fellow he works for has it in for you."

"That's not news. But what about I.L.C.?"

"Percy says this fellow—Limedecker, or whatever it is, has plans to get I.L.C. to come and see your plant. Bid on it. All on the sly, you understand. L.E. wants to merge with G.E. They hope they can get you out with the zoning plan, force it so you have to sell to I.L.C. Percy says the Industrial Development Committee won't be sympathetic with you if you get an offer from I.L.C., and your likelihood of swinging a loan in these parts will be unlikely, if you know what I mean, if you got an offer from I.L.C. . . . That make sense?"

"Yes, it makes sense," said Slater Burr.

"Percy says Leydecker will stop at nothing to get you out! He says it's like an obsession with him, getting you out of town!"

"Is that it?"

"Yes. Do I get my fifty now?"

Slater pointed to the money, and the young man scooped it up.

"Is this the way you live?" Slater said.

"It's the way I earn travelling expenses sometimes, when I'm stuck in a small town like this. I head for the Y.M.C.A., sort of a home office."

"And that's where you met Oliver Percy?"

"He goes there to—swim," the young man snickered.

"You don't look queer," Slater Burr said.

"I'm not. *Me* queer? Would you take me for a faggot?"

"I don't know what I'd take you for," said Slater, buttoning his coat, "but I know I'd a hell of a lot rather be taken for queer than taken for you!"

Whoom! Carrie's explosive laughter; oh, Mr. High and Mighty, is evil so offensive to your delicate sensitivities? And he laughed inwardly at himself, waiting until the young man was gone; how coolly he had said those words: I'd a hell of a lot rather . . . Whoom! Whoom!

But Fate was often an unsuspecting ally. He knew it as he picked the phone off its cradle and made the call to Miss Rae; let there be a strike over Sontag and Secora, it was all part of the scheme of things; only Miss Rae knew better, knew that he had fired them in a clap of fury, and he would tell her they were not to be rehired, she was not to try and reach them. Her telephone did not answer; when he got home, he would call her again.

And when he got home, he knew even more how easily Fate often cooperated. In the kitchen he made himself a martini, waiting for Jen to finish her tirade.

". . . makes you look guilty, that's what I'm concerned about—firing them that way, all over asinine gossip!" she said.

He said, "Jenny, how well do you know me?"

"I'm beginning to wonder."

"Do you *ever* listen when I talk about business?"

"Slater, it has nothing to do with . . ."

"Just listen to me, Jenny. Please?" a little smile playing at his lips. "I fired them because I want a strike! I couldn't just fire two people for no reason; it'd *look* as though I wanted a strike. Jenny, I chose them because it'll seem as though anger motivated me . . . Oh, I'll be forced to rehire them, no doubt of that, but for awhile there'll be plenty of trouble at the plant."

"What do you mean?"

And he told her about Leydecker and Ithaca Lock. He watched while her expression changed from one of anxiety to one of admiration, then love, in the softness of her eyes, the release of her full lips from their tightness, the beautiful, soft countenance of calm.

"Now do you see?" he said.

"But you were angry when you left this morning. I'd never seen you so angry."

"Yes. I collected my thoughts in the car, on the way to the office . . . You see, Jenny, everything works out." . . . Whoom!

. . . Well, Carrie, it does; lookit me, hmmm? He said to Jen, "Is Cloward in the living room?"

"Yes . . . Slater, I'm sorry."

"Oh, God, don't apologize! Business is complicated, Jenny."

"You had me scared. For awhile I was even . . ."

"Even what?"

She laughed. "Oh, well . . . I let Donald drive, coming out here?"

"Yes?"

"He had trouble starting the car—the shift, you know?"

"And for awhile you began to think I was the bogy man, hmm?"

"It did frighten me a little. On top of that, Miss Sontag calling, and everything."

"Yes, well, he probably had trouble with the shift the night he killed Carrie too . . . You know, Jenny, I think you're right. I'm not much on parlor psychology, never liked it, but I think you're right. I probably did feel some guilt about Carrie's death. I suppose it's only natural."

"Of course, it is, darling."

"Yes, well, I'll be glad when Cloward's out of here."

"And so will I! Slater, I love you."

"Je t'adore."

"It still always sounds like 'shut the door' when you say it."

"I wish we could go upstairs and shut the bedroom door."

"Take a raincheck, will you? For about eleven-thirty to-night?"

"You're on."

"Slater, I feel so much better! Oh, darling!"

And it was fine between them again; the Martini just right too; a giddy glow of euphoria all through Slater Burr, with the explosive sounds of Carrie's laughter far, far in the background.

II.

"I'm sorry about my cousin, sir," said Ted Chayka. "I took him to his place, and I got my wife to go over there, keep him home for the night."

"Yes, that's best. I want to do what's best for the town, do you understand me, Chayka?"

"I certainly do, Mr. Leydecker."

"Your cousin has quite an imagination."

"You mean the stuff about Slater Burr killing his wife?"

"Yes."

"I don't blame Mr. Burr for firing him."

"It wasn't because of Secora's idiotic talk, Ted. It's a bit more complicated. Slater Burr is above that . . . No, I trace it all to Oliver Percy."

"*What*, sir?"

"It's too involved. But you see Percy is a braggart. He gets puffed up with importance . . . Now, he dates Donald Cloward's sister. He's told me a few times that he takes her out . . . I think he's been telling her my business, showing off the fact he's in on many very personal and discreet business relations . . . I think he told her, and she told her brother, and word got back to Burr through the Cloward boy."

Chayka did not understand, but he nodded as though he did.

Leydecker said, "It was very nice of you to come here and deliver Cloward's message . . . I'm sorry you got involved in all this other business."

"Oh, that's all right, sir."

"I know a policeman doesn't make much, and I'm happy to reimburse you for your time."

"Please, Mr. Leydecker, I wouldn't think of it."

"I want to reimburse you . . . and there's something else."

"I don't want any money from you, sir."

"Never mind protesting, Ted . . . I want to give you something. And," Leydecker looked at his wrist watch, "it's quarter to eight now . . . I want you to do something else for me."

"Certainly, sir."

"Secora claims Cloward is at Slater Burr's."

"Yes, sir."

"I want you to call there and tell Cloward that I'd like to talk with him. Here in my office. At nine-thirty tonight. Tell him personally. Tell him it's about Laura."

"Yes, sir. I'll do that."

"You see, Chayka, my daughter is very ill. I can't trust Cloward. I can't know for sure he won't go to my house tonight and upset her."

"I think I can promise you he won't."

"Think isn't good enough. I don't want him near my house."

"I see."

"I'm going to tell Cloward in plain English that he'll find himself in plenty of trouble, if he goes near my house. Oh, I'm going to be nice to him. I want to check out Percy through him too, confirm my suspicions on that count . . . The important thing is that Cloward comes here at nine-thirty."

"I'll call him right now, sir."

"I'd appreciate that," Leydecker said. "And something else, Chayka. You don't go on duty until eleven or so, do you?"

"No."

"I'd like you to go by my house about nine-thirty, just in case there's any slip-up, do you see? I'll give you $50."

"That isn't necess——"

"Never mind protesting, Ted. I like you. I think you're going to amount to something!"

"Thank you, Mr. Leydecker. I certainly want to. I'll call Cloward right now, sir."

III.

Yes, lamb, I'll take care of everything, GRanite 2846, for the hundredth time, but O lamb, I don't care.

"Hello?"

"Mr. Secora?"

"Yeah."

"Mr. Secora, this is Miss Rae, Mr. Burr's secretary."

"How's it hanging?"

"What?"

She could hear laughter in the background; Oh, Al, she could hear, what a thing to say!

He was guffawing as he spoke, "You'll understand it in your next life, Miss Rae, when you come back a man." More laughter.

"Mr. Secora?"

"Yeah, what's up? To what do I owe this crappy honor?"

But *she* could take the abuse; for you, lamb, *anything!*

She said, "Mr. Burr is sorry. You still have your job, Mr. Secora. It was just a little fit of temper."

"Oh, just a little fit of temper, hah?"

"That's all," she said cheerily. "We all have them. But you will be paid for today, and you still have your job."

"Miss Rae?"

"Yes?"

"When you go to work tomorrow, you tell your Mr. Burr that he can shove his job! You tell him that he can take his f——ing job and——" Miss Rae clamped down the phone's arm, shaking, her ears burning with the obscenities Albert Secora had begun to shout.

IV.

"I don't get it, Buzzy," said Slater Burr. "Why would Chayka give you a message from Leydecker?"

They were all sitting at the dining room table. Jen Burr had answered the phone, and called Cloward away from the table. Cloward poked at his lemon pie and shrugged. "I guess he just ran into Leydecker, Mr. Burr." . . . Above all, he was not going to be trapped into a confession of last night's drunken folly. Not just when everything was going along smoothly.

"I just don't get it! Chayka's a policeman. What's Leydecker calling in a policeman for?"

"Ted and I went to Industrial High together, Mr. Burr. I think Mr. Leydecker probably remembers that, and thought we'd be running into each other."

If he did not keep the appointment with Leydecker, there was a chance Leydecker would call the Burrs himself, perhaps spill the whole story; then Slater Burr would know he was still foolish and back in the past . . . There was another reason he wanted to meet with Leydecker . . . not *just* curiosity about Laura, but back to the old fantasy. *"You and I both know the truth, Donald, and I'm ready to make it up to you."* . . . Let all of them make it up to him, if they wanted to. Let them all feel big as hell to forgive Donald Cloward; big little gods, *let* them!

Slater Burr said, "Forget it! That's my advice—forget it!"

"Mr. Burr?"

"What?"

"I want to see him. The train doesn't go until eleven. I could still see him and catch the train. What would it hurt?"

Jen Burr said, "I'd be curious to know what he wants."

"Oh, the hell with it! He's got a policeman in on it, he probably wants trouble for you, Buzz!"

He could not tell Slater Burr how Ted got in on it, without giving it away. Ted had said "He's not going to make trouble for you, Buzz—honest he isn't. He just wants to talk to you."

Cloward said, "He's not going to make trouble for me."

"How can you be so sure, Buzz?" said Slater Burr. "Remember, you're on parole."

"But I didn't do anything," Cloward lied. He looked hard at Jen, hoping she would not give away the fact he had phoned the Leydeckers last night.

Jen Burr said, "He'd still make his train, Slater. Maybe he wants to tell Donald what happened to Laura. I wouldn't mind knowing that myself!"

"Listen!" Slater Burr was shouting. "You asked for my help, Buzz! Now you want me to help you! I told you to stay away from the Leydeckers! I'll put you on the 11 o'clock and that's that!"

"I said I'd be there, Mr. Burr. I want to go."

"What'll it harm, Slater?" Jen said.

V.

He watched Jen light a Gauloise, put it in her mouth and begin clearing the table, with the cigarette dangling there from her lips. He could hear more whooms! and he shut them out with effort, trying now to think through the haze of alcohol and the noise of china rattling as Jen stacked the plates. Jen never walked around with a cigarette hanging from her mouth, and what was a policeman calling Buzzy Cloward for, to deliver a message from Leydecker; cockeyed; he had to think straight, just for a few more hours. He could offer to drive Buzzy to the Leydeckers, take the back road, pull the choke out and flood the engine; invent motor trouble . . . Delay it . . . How long could he do that? . . . Or, when he got Buzzy in the car, he could reason with him, frighten him with remembrances of the past, and how Leydecker hated him . . . That was okay . . . a drink somewhere, get the kid loaded. That was okay. He would have to handle it just right. Whoom! . . . and Jen with the cigarette that way, as though for an instant of time, Carrie had gotten inside her, was pushing her to encourage Cloward to meet with Leydecker . . . But what did Leydecker want? . . . Secora had gone to him, told him the story; Leydecker wanted to hear more, wanted Ted Chayka to hear more . . . If Buzzy Cloward just skipped out, his story would not hold up . . . just hot air. Leydecker and Chayka would see that.

Jen said, "Slater, what are you frowning about?"

"Was I?"

Cloward said, "Mr. Leydecker probably just wants to warn me not to go near Laura."

Jen winked at Cloward, as though she and Cloward had some little secret all their own. "I think so too," she said. "I think that's all he wants."

And the most impossible, crazy ideas began spinning through Slater's mind: a trap was being set for him. Jen had seen that the kid could not operate the Jaguar immediately; Jen was in on it. Whoom! and again.

Slater said, "Have a brandy, Buzz. We'll have some brandy."

"There isn't time," said Jen. "It's eight o'clock. Donald will want to wash up!"

"What?" Slater looked at her, as though she were the enemy there with the Gauloise hanging off her lips. "Not *time?* It's an hour and a half away!"

"I think Mrs. Burr means that I shouldn't drink, sir."

Jen smiled at him. "Ummm hmmm."

What the hell was going on! And the whooms came like distant thunder, and through it all the phone ringing again . . . ringing, ringing, and Jen saying, "Get it, Donald, hmmm? It's right behind you."

twenty-one

"That was fun!" said Nancy Chayka. "You're fun, Al. Ted's turned into a namby-pamby."

"If I'd gotten Slater Burr, I was just going to tell him: f--- your job! You ain't going to buy me off with your job, not any more!"

"S'afternoon, Al, Francie Boyson tells me the whole story, see? But she doesn't say how *she* knows, see? 'I can't say how I know,' she says, 'but I know.' "

"Sure, she knows. We was hunting the same kinda thing in the same hunting ground as Slater Burr and Jen Mc-Kenzie. Boy, I don't know why the bells didn't ring a long time ago, when Mrs. Burr got killed."

Nancy Chayka peeled off another nail, sitting there on the couch beside Albert Secora, in his apartment. She said, "What'd the Cloward kid say?"

"Well, I says, who is this, and he says this is Donald Cloward, see?"

"Yeah, I heard *that*."

"So, I says, If I was you, Cloward, I'd get the hell out of that place before Slater Burr kills you too, I says."

"I know, I heard *that*."

"I says, You're a sitting duck, Buzzy! It was Slater Burr driving that car, I says, and nobody else. I figured it out, I says, and I hit it right, because I got fired today for what I know, and then he tried to rehire me, Buzz. Oh, the heat's on him, Buzz! I says, He don't want to help you, he wants you out of town. You just happened to come near the truth yesterday, only not near enough."

"Yeah, well, what'd he say?"

"He didn't say nothing. I says, Are you listening? and he says, 'Yes.' "

"Then?"

"Then I just told him. I says, Slater Burr and his dear whore wife was sleeping around *before* that so-called accident, and he wanted the first Mrs. Burr out of his life. I just told him. *You* heard me."

"What'd he say?"

"Nothing. He just hung up."

"Just hung up, hah?"

"Yeah . . . Hey, I had enough coffee. Let's have a drink."

"I'm supposed to baby-sit with you. You're not supposed to drink."

"Oh yeah? Sez who?" he laughed, putting his hand on her arm. He ran it down her arm to her skirt.

"You're fun," she said.

"Yeah, and I think we can have us some fun, Nancy. Get us a little snort, sort of oil us up for some fun."

twenty-two

He knew in an instant that it was true, an instant that closed the gap between doubt and knowing, while Slater Burr came around to get inside the car where he was sitting, still unsure, until he realized what song Slater Burr was humming. *Hey there, you with the stars in your eyes.*

Fear began to sift down from his brain in fine sands, then became heavy pressure, and wave after wave of it swept through him, while Slater Burr started the engine.

Slater Burr said, "What was that phone call all about anyway, the last one?"

"I told you. I couldn't understand. A drunk or something."

"But you said 'yes' at one point. What'd you say 'yes' to?" They turned down the drive, and soon they would be alone in the night.

"Someone, whoever it was, said— I don't remember. Something about it being the wrong number. Yes, they asked me if they had the wrong number."

"They?"

"He did."

"Who, Buzz?"

"I don't know. Honestly."

"I see." And again, the song; only now he was whistling it. They cut across the black road leading from the Burr house, onto a side road . . . not the highway, which would take them right into Cayuta.

Slater Burr said, "What're you so nervous about?"

"I'm not."

"Playing with your comb that way."

"Oh, that's just a habit. I'm sorry."

"Nothing to be nervous about, Buzzy."

"Yes, sir."

They drove along in silence. He kept whistling the song. Cloward was perspiring now, his clothes soaked. Then the engine sputtered.

Slater Burr said, "Oh, oh."

"Something wrong?" Cloward managed.

"I better stop and have a look at the motor."

"Yes, sir."

"Hope we don't run into trouble out here. It's so damn far from anything."

He stopped the car and got out.

While he was looking under the hood, Cloward reached for a cigarette. It would be impossible to run. He could never run fast enough; Slater Burr could catch him. He fumbled for a match, but found none in his pockets. He snapped open the glove compartment and saw the gun. Quickly, he took the gun. He could think of nothing to do with it, and he saw Slater Burr walking back to the car, so he sat on it.

"I'm afraid we have some motor trouble. It might take awhile to fix it."

"Yes, sir."

"What's the matter with you?"

"What do you mean?"

"Your hand's shaking."

"I don't know. I—"

"What is it, Buzzy?"

He threw the cigarette out the window, eased his hands back by the seat of his trousers.

Slater Burr said, "What the hell's the matter with you?"

His right hand gripped the gun firmly, and he pulled his hand out from under him and pointed the gun at Slater Burr.

"What the devil?"

"You take me into town, Mr. Burr. I'll kill you, if you don't."

"I told you the car's in trouble. Now, don't be a fool!"

"I'll kill you, Mr. Burr," Cloward repeated. "You're not going to kill me."

"Buzzy, I don't want to . . ." and he moved toward Cloward, and Cloward felt his hands on his shoulders again, familiar . . . and his finger squeezed the trigger.

twenty-three

"*That's all the facts when you come to brass tacks,*" Mrs. Basso read, "*Birth and*— Laura, I really think this is not a very *nice* poem!"

"It was your idea to read to me, Mrs. Basso," Laura sighed.

"Well, I never suggested this sort of reading!"

"Then stop reading to me. Go home."

"I was just waiting until your pills took and you got sleepy."

"*Birth and copulation and death,*" Laura Leydecker recited. "*I've been born and once is enough. . . .* Is the word copulation offensive, Mrs. Basso?"

"The entire poem is offensive, Laura." Mrs. Basso flicked through the pages. "*You've had a cream of a nightmare dream, and you've got the hoo-ha's coming to you. Hoo Hoo Hoo . . .* It's not even poetry. I don't like it at all!"

"Why don't you just go home, Mrs. Basso."

"You know the whole thing by heart anyway."

"So I do."

"Why should I read it to you? Really, Laura, you ought to try to pull yourself together. Your poor father is frantic."

"Then go down to L.E. and sit with him, Mrs. Basso."

"And you haven't eaten . . ."

"No, and I won't eat until you go home . . . It's nine o'clock."

"Oh, I'm leaving, have no fear of that. I just hoped your pills would take before I left."

Laura Leydecker said, "You don't like me at all, do you, Mrs. Basso?"

"I love you, Laura, and my heart goes out to you, but you don't try. A girl like you, wasting away here, making those grotesque clay dolls, and watching the television until your eyes are red . . . Reading this sort of book! . . . You need to get out!"

"And be laughed at, Mrs. Basso? Be ridiculed?"

"Mrs. John F. Kennedy wears a wig when she goes to parties. I read it in the newspaper."

"Well, I don't feel like becoming the town spectacle, Mrs. Basso. I had enough of that when I was younger. At least this way, nobody knows what to laugh at. I hope they think I've taken to the bottle!"

"What an awful thing to say, Laura."

"Would you rather be a drunk or bald, Mrs. Basso?"

"Why, when Jack Paar was on the Tonight Show, he'd even brag he had a hairpiece," Mrs. Basso said.

"Mrs. Basso, I'm tired."

"Your pills are working. Thank heaven!"

"I'm not just tired that way. I'm tired of all this talk about all these celebrities who have wigs. I don't care to hear any more of it. If I have to hear any more of it, you'll have to hear my kind of talk. Do you understand me?"

"Don't start your disgusting talk with me, Laura. Bad enough you read this trash . . . this T.S. Eliot, without your talk too."

"Give me my book back, and go home, please."

"That's exactly what I intend to do, Laura."

Laura Leydecker sank her head back into the soft pillows and waited while she heard Mrs. Basso's footsteps descending on the back stairs. Then the rattle of the garbage can, as she took the brown paper bag from it for deposit in the bin outside, on her way from the Leydeckers . . . then the shutting of the kitchen door.

A drowsiness fought her hunger, and she lay there for awhile, until hunger won over. She got up and slipped on the old robe, went down the long hallway, and down the stairs.

Whatever the pills were she had taken, they were more effective than the others, over which she had built a certain immunity, so that it took three, sometimes four to put her to sleep. These sleeping pills had tranquilizers mixed in. *I love tranquil solitude, and such society, as is quiet,* ah but f--- tranquillity, she thought, and she thought all the other words he had ever taught her, and put them in legion against tranquillity; ah God, f---- tranquillity, and she looked in the icebox for something there to eat.

She did not even turn on the kitchen light, because f--- the kitchen light, as well, and all light. She had read somewhere that even the blind turned on the lights in their homes, to better appease those with sight, to seem more like them

. . . well, that had not been her luck, to seem like anyone, but a bald old crow, and she gave a little laugh, a little tipsy laugh—that was what those pills did to her, and by the light of the icebox she found a brick of cheese. She left the door open on the refrigerator, holding it with her leg, gnawing on the cheese, a bald old mouse, alone in the night, *life goes on forever like the gnawing of a mouse* . . . but it seemed then suddenly, very suddenly, that Edna St. Vincent Millay was terribly, terribly wrong: life did not go on forever: life had an end, and Laura Leydecker realized it, so quickly, and so suddenly, that she barely touched her fingers around to her back, after the crack of a gun, after the beginnings of blood warm down her flesh; life did not go on forever, for in an instant the mouse was dead.

twenty-four

He fired three times to be certain.

He watched while Leydecker slumped to the kitchen floor; he had hit him clean and accurately.

Quickly, he wiped his prints from the gun, and with his gloves, placed the gun back in Cloward's hand, easing out the stick he had put in its place, while he drove Cloward's corpse to the Leydecker house.

Cloward's body was slumped across the porch, where Slater had dragged him, the hole in his head still oozing blood, which was smeared across Slater's overcoat.

He had not wanted to kill Cloward; the gun had gone off in their struggle for possession of it. If he had not killed him, he would be dead, that was certain.

There was not even time to figure everything out, but he felt a certain thrill at his own quick thinking, and his thoughts were still spinning, weaving the story, coming in bullet-like succession. Cloward had insisted on keeping his appointment with Leydecker. Slater had noticed a certain sullenness as he drove him to Leydecker's. No, he had not even been aware of Cloward taking the gun from his glove compartment; he always carried the gun, target practice . . . and Slater could see himself standing in the police station, logical and concerned, he had always liked the kid, sent him a Christmas card every year; yes, he would say, he was at my house for dinner . . . Jen and I . . . and then, starting down the walk as he went over all of it, he realized he would be put to the test sooner than he had planned . . . much sooner . . . Now!

"Mr. Burr?"

"Yes . . . Is it *you*, Chayka?"

They came into the circle of light from the street lamp, at the side of Leydecker's house.

Chayka was out of breath. "I heard a gun. I came running. I was just at the corner."

"It's too late," Slater said. *Whoom!* But he stayed steady, facing Chayka, letting the pieces fit into place. There, it was coming out, his words, clearly, not a shred of hesitation. "I'm afraid it's just too late."

"What happened?"

"Donald Cloward was at my house tonight. He had an appointment with Mr. Leydecker and—" but Chayka did not wait for him to finish. He ran toward the house.

Another lucky break. Slater thought of the blood in his car. He would have to get rid of the blood, and he hurried toward the car, realizing even as he went through the motions, that he could not wipe it away. He would have to explain it away. That was it. Let me just explain; let me just pull myself together and explain . . . and he leaned against his car, his heart banging against his chest, those crazy, mocking explosions of laughter aggravating his thoughts; oh God, let me just explain it . . . But there you were, Ted Chayka was walking toward him again, and he felt his nerves rev up, felt himself take hold.

"It's too late, isn't it?" he said. There was a sliver's chance, of course, that Leydecker was still alive . . . but that sliver was removed with Ted's answer. "Yes . . . too late. Do you want to tell me about it, Mr. Burr?"

"Certainly," Slater said. "I suppose you were to be here at nine-thirty too, hmm?"

"Yes. I was supposed to be here."

"Well, you're right on time . . . Unfortunately we were early."

"What happened, Mr. Burr?"

"Donald Cloward had this appointment with Leydecker. You know that. I think you delivered the message."

"Yes."

"Well, Cloward got nervous. I thought it was nervousness. He wanted to be a little early, he said. Kept asking me if my car could go any faster, you know?" the words were pouring out, easy, natural, and Chayka stood there watching him respectfully, listening. "I let him out. I thought he was a little sullen. I thought I'd wait for a minute and see how things went . . . Then maybe I'd get a fast one at Rich Boyson's, and come back for him, if things seemed all right."

"Yes . . . Well, we better start on to the police station. You can tell me about it in the car," Chayka said. "We have to make a report."

"Certainly. I'm glad to cooperate. There's blood in my car. After Cloward killed Leydecker, he came running out to me. I said, 'Donald, you have to turn yourself in. I can't help you.' They'd had some sort of argument." That was bad . . . the part about blood on Cloward. There were ways of testing blood; that was a mistake. But if the police believed him, would they bother to check? Whoom again; all right, but wait . . . wait and watch me work this.

Chayka said, "We can take my car. I parked it around the corner."

"Just leave mine here, hmm?"

"I think that's best."

"Certainly . . . Anything to cooperate." . . . Jen . . . He could call Jen; tell her to pick up the car, wash it with ammonia . . . no, don't ask questions; go and get it . . . meanwhile, he would cooperate.

They walked toward the head of Highland Hill.

Chayka said, "Then Cloward killed Leydecker, is that it?"

"Yes . . . Then he killed himself. I couldn't stop him. He ran from my car, back to the porch. He killed himself."

"I see."

"He shot him through the window." God, he had almost forgotten that; good, he had remembered . . . No, oh, God, it was full of holes. Let me think. Whoom! Whoom!, and in the street light's amber glow, Carrie's face, smoke spiraling up, curling around the leer on her face like a snake coiling to spring out at him.

Chayka said, "I made a call to the police."

"They had a fight, you see. Leydecker ordered him out of the house, or something. I couldn't understand the kid—he was so hysterical. But I heard them shouting at one another in there."

"I see . . . My car's over there."

"He shot him through the window, on his way out of the house. I don't know what was said between them. Did you have any idea what it was all about?"

"No," said Chayka.

"I told him that he'd have to turn himself in . . . Well, I guess he took that way out—shooting himself . . . He ran back, and I heard the gun go off again."

"Make sure your door's closed, Mr. Burr," Chayka said.

"Well, Ted," said Slater Burr, "it's pretty horrible, isn't it? Are there any questions you want to ask?"

"No . . . I'm off-duty."

"What did Leydecker want with the kid?"

"I think he just wanted to make sure Buzzy stayed away from Laura."

"Then that's probably what the fight was about."

"Umm hmm."

They turned onto Genesee, a silence between them for several long minutes, while Slater tried to think it through; no, it was best not to send Jen for the car. Leave the car; if they believed him . . .

He said, "It sounds pretty unbelievable, doesn't it, Ted?"

"It's a strange world, Mr. Burr."

Good! "Yes, a strange world . . . You never know what will happen next . . . Poor kid, though, I feel sorry for him. I even feel sorry for Leydecker, and you know," a brave little chuckle, "we never got along, Ted. I mean, we weren't good friends."

"I know that."

"But I wouldn't wish him anything like this. Shot in the back that way." Oh my God, that was dumb! Whoom! Dumb! He said, "Donald told me he shot him in the back."

"Umm hmm, well . . . It's a strange world."

He began to get a weak feeling as they pulled in at the police station . . . a suspicious air of calm enveloped the place as he walked in with Chayka. Chayka pointed to a chair and asked him to wait a moment. He sat down, blood all over his overcoat; explain *that* by saying he had run back at the gunshot, pulled Cloward to him, hoping the kid was still alive; why every year I sent him a Christmas card—whoom! and now he heard a man's voice curt with anger. ". . . don't just leave two bodies and come running with . . ." and he caught no more. Mumbling and another angry sound . . . Slater Burr waited. Then his face broke into a grin. Lieutenant Cheever! He knew Cheever very well; he used to buy Cheever drinks, take him across to Rich Boyson's when Cheever stopped by the plant. Cheever was okay; good!

He stood up and smiled at Cheever. "Hello, Lieutenant."

"Hello, Mr. Burr. I hear there's been some trouble."

"Yes. It's terrible! . . . There was this shouting argument between Leydecker and Cloward, and . . . has Ted filled you in? There was this really . . ."

Cheever interrupted. "Let's go into my office," he said.

Slater said, "Yes. Yes, I can help clear the whole thing up, I think."

"You say you heard Leydecker and Cloward shouting?"

"I should have interceded, but . . ."

"To the left," Lieutenant Cheever directed him.

Slater smiled at the Lieutenant. It was reassuring to see Cheever, out of it all to see so familiar a face, one he could count on for sympathy, understanding; *I thought the world of that kid . . . no, not too exaggerated.* He had killed Carrie, remember, *that kid. . . .* Watch me work it, Carrie, he thought, and as Cheever beckoned him toward his office, Slater felt a tickle of elation: oh he'd come through, he would . . . he *would.*

Then from the far end of the station, a figure hurrying through the door, scrambling like a cat with its tail on fire, toward Slater and the Lieutenant, and Slater stared at another familiar face, oh very, very familiar . . . The face of Kenneth Leydecker.

That was the biggest whoom of them all.

THE END
of an Original Gold Medal Novel by
Vin Packer